D1420114

Vladimir Makanin

Escape Hatch
&
The Long Road Ahead

Two Novellas

Translated & with an Afterword
by
Mary Ann Szporluk

Ardis, Dana Point

PRINTED IN THE UNITED STATES OF AMERICA

ARDIS PUBLISHERS
24721 EL CAMINO CAPISTRANO
DANA POINT, CA 92629

First Paperback Edition 1997
ISBN 0-375-70108-7

Library of Congress Cataloging-in-Publication Data

Makanin, Vladimir.
[Laz. English]
Escape hatch : two novellas / by Vladimir Makanin : translated by Mary Ann Szporluk.
p. cm.
Contents: Escape hatch -- The long road ahead.
ISBN 0-87501-110-1 : $24.00
1. Makanin, Vladimir--Translations into English. I. Makanin, Vladimir. The long road ahead. 1995. II. Title
PG3483.2K27A27 1995

94-7869
CIP

891.73'44–dc20

Contents

Escape Hatch

1

A HESITANT CAT IS AT THE DOOR. On the threshold itself, in fact. Not coming in and not going out. So, of course, he can't close the door. "Well?... In or out?" The tone of his voice rouses the cat, and then Klyucharyov slams the door of the apartment and quickly runs down the stairs. He passes the cat (springing softly down step by step) and goes outside.

Suddenly he thinks about his friend Pavlov. How did he die? What were the details?... He doesn't know a thing. Two hundred people had died in a mob, caught and crushed in its rush—and that's if you just count the ones on the boulevard. The mob doesn't count. (But Pavlov hadn't been there, anyway.)

Klyucharyov tries not to think about the fact that no one is on the street now and many people are hiding in their apartments behind thickly curtained windows. Of course, it is a little scary without people. But without people there isn't any danger, either. It is warm on the street. It's getting dark, but not yet night. The street is so warm you feel that any moment now a whistle will shriek and a mob of them will run out, bringing murders and muggings along with them, and the weak will be trampled—this feeling is so heavy, how can you keep your spirits up? But right now the street is empty. It's quiet. And this, too, is life... The sensitive, frightened thoughts of an intellectual waver back and forth like this while Klyucharyov himself steps along.

If you look down at it now, the city is deserted—there are no people, no cars moving along the streets (a few individual cars parked lifelessly at the side of the road just emphasize the general absence of motion). The sidewalks are empty. A single man moves along the glassy street, wearing a sweater and a cap with a pompon. The pompon almost bounces as he walks. It's Klyucharyov, an old acquaintance of ours. (He has aged some, he's a little paler, his temples are quite gray and there are patches of gray in his hair. But he is still strong. A man.)

As he walks, he periodically makes a strange twitching movement with his body, as if beneath his sweater and shirt there's a wound on his side that hasn't healed completely (and there is; there are several wounds, in fact). The thin knit cap with the pompon (it resembles a ski cap) is pulled down tightly on his head. Crowning his ordinary sweater and pants, the ski cap gives him a somewhat eccentric look. (Klyucharyov wouldn't agree with this. For him the cap expresses the logical evolution of his intellectual makeup; it is both a modest provocation and a protective form. But it isn't mimicry.)

When Klyucharyov passes the third five-story building, there really is a whistle. Klyucharyov comes to a stop. He looks around. No, not a soul in sight. (Well, why not, someone might just whistle.)

He passes a row of level five-story apartment buildings, continues down a familiar asphalt path and comes to an empty lot. The lot turns into a field overgrown with grass and weeds, and the paved path becomes an ordinary narrow path which loops its way through the grass. The path is still easy to see. Over there are the tall clusters of two sorrel shrubs. Klyucharyov walks up to a narrow gap in the earth, to the hatch, as he has christened it; he usually stamps his feet so that he won't drag any extra dirt with him into the hole. (When it rains, he scrapes the mud off on the coarse grass. But it's not raining, thank God.)

Klyucharyov puts his legs into the hole and sits for a while trying to decide whether to go in. Then he lowers himself, or, to be more exact, pushes himself in. His body rubs against the sides and the roughness scratches him, but his skin isn't scraped. (Sometimes it's very easy to get through the hole.) And now, just after thinking how easy it is to go down and forgetting to be careful, Klyucharyov hits a sharp stone jutting out and rips the scab off the old wound on his side. Damn it! His shirt is instantly wet—blood, of course. The buttons torn off the shirt fall down. Klyucharyov has only worked his way down to the narrowest part (mid-way), but his buttons fly far ahead and you can hear them clink at the bottom. The neck is narrow. Klyucharyov's body makes an agile turning motion and he twists around, catching his breath for a moment because of the tightness, but only for a moment, and then he's through—and now his body is hanging over a cavernous space, not over darkness, though, but over the brightly lit space of a rather large hall filled with tables where people are sitting and talking and drinking wine.

Putting his feet on metal rungs, Klyucharyov climbs down a stairway (something like a tall stepladder), and finds himself inside a beautiful room with an enormous, bright checkered floor. The entire floor is covered with large white and dark squares. When he reaches the bottom, Klyucharyov steps on one of the squares and immediately finds two of his buttons.

The bar in this wine cellar is noisy: people are drinking and talking. (What Klyucharyov really needs is a shovel, a good ordinary shovel with a smooth handle, but he can't just run off and buy it right away, needless to say.) He sees Andrei Bashkin, Severyanych, and Tanya Yeremeyeva; they're waving to him. Not only do they look alike, they share a kindred spirit. Klyucharyov has to walk past them, no matter what. Their waves seem to be sincere; they're signaling him to come and sit with them a while (Nuances!—but you can never be certain about anything here), so Klyucharyov goes over, he's glad to see them too. They pour him a glass of wine, greet him gaily and noisily, and push over a bowl of nuts. "So how are you? How's life up there?... Maybe you'd like to join us and talk a little?" they ask almost in unison, knowing how drawn he is to conversation.

"I would. I'd love to!" he gives the obvious answer to the obvious question, and they all laugh at the same time, having anticipated it.

"That a boy! Terrific!... Great to see you! Sit down!... What'll you drink?"

They find him a chair right away (after a friendly exchange with someone and some jokes, they pull over a chair from the next table). Klyucharyov wasn't planning to sit with them, but he does sit down, of course; he's happy to be sitting there, holding a glass in his hands, and he takes large sips of the dark wine (the wine is a little cold and he warms it with his hands). He listens to the ongoing conversation about the nature of their modern society: is it a community or a cooperative?... A community has very deep roots, but a cooperative is a work association. Klyucharyov only listens superficially, he's just enjoying the social conversation he misses so much, and then Nikodimov appears at the table, as preoccupied as ever. He puts a friendly hand on Klyucharyov's shoulder and leans down (so that he can speak quietly): "Let's go, Viktor. I promise you we'll only be there for a minute."

Klyucharyov quickly throws two nuts in his mouth. Lightly salted and carefully shelled. Klyucharyov would like to sit there longer, but Nikodimov pleads: "Vitya, I promised to bring you as soon as you showed up. Come on, help me out. Don't let me down."

Klyucharyov nods to this group he finds so pleasant and intelligent–as if to say, I'll be back. Klyucharyov and Nikodimov set off together and walk the entire length of the wine cellar, navigating between tables, and when they exit they turn into a long corridor with splendid soft lighting. It's always light here, it's like being outside on a bright day. And it's done with such taste and artistry that you can't even tell where the light is coming from. Nikodimov walks one step ahead. Ah, there's the office. Klyucharyov feels that he's following Nikodimov into the editorial office without the slightest desire; and, without the slightest desire, he'll also end up saying something there. This isn't anything he needs. What he needs is a shovel. An ordinary shovel. Ridiculous, isn't it?

They enter through a revolving door. Nikodimov simply says "He's with me" to the guard and leads Klyucharyov in.

WE'll BE HAPPY FOR ANY INFORMATION. That's what they said. On all sides there are shelves of books. A young woman behind a typewriter. A telex rattling in a corner, automatically registering information from the outside. And two men at a desk. Both of them are turning gray. When Nikodimov and Klyucharyov enter, the two journalists rise from their swivel chairs. They identify themselves.

And Nikodimov gives the name of the person he has brought (invited): "Klyucharyov."

"Yes, yes," they both nod cordially. They seem interested.

"We're pleased," they say, "we're very pleased you've come, and remember that we appreciate any information you have. After all, we live in the same country, even though we're cut off from each other at present, because of the restrictive conditions we're under. That's just how things have turned out. But we're suffering, you know. Your life up there is our life too—try to understand us correctly..." Klyucharyov understands. (He nods to indicate his honest agreement and understanding.)

He understands (and is slightly annoyed: what if they offer him money? But they're too tactful. Besides, they know that money doesn't mean very much out on the darkening city streets). When Klyucharyov first walked in, he was undoubtedly just an item of business for them—pure business. But now their faces can't hide their dismay. They don't know what to ask. And suddenly they're asking (in pained voices): Are there dead bodies on the streets, are the dead just lying there, has Klyucharyov seen any?

"I haven't," he answers.

The conversation dries up. Klyucharyov nods and walks off. One of them runs after Klyucharyov, quickly catches up to him and as a way of parting says that once he lived in Mnevniki himself, almost in the center of town, on the Taganka, during his early years there—he can see his two old streets right now.

After Klyucharyov leaves with Nikodimov, who is quite happy with their visit, Klyucharyov's mind (which until now has been completely lucid) becomes confused. His eyes can't find anything to fix upon. The revolving door through which they've just come keeps on turning; the door becomes enormous and now it's turning so slowly, so smoothly... "Viktor!..." he hears Nikodimov's scream, but somehow the scream is far away. He almost falls. He grabs onto the doorpost of a building, then straightens up and takes leave of Nikodimov. "Goodbye, Viktor." "Take care."

But as soon as Klyucharyov turns the corner, he feels sick again, and only now does he realize that he's dizzy and that the wound in his side hurts so much. "I have to go to a clinic," he tells himself. There's a drugstore on every corner here. There must be a first-aid clinic nearby.

Here the streetlamps are the old-fashioned kind, not those poles with bent necks and cobra heads. The small lamps are tightly fitted, almost stuck, to the walls, and they hang in antique lantern frames from the splendid days of Pushkin. They emit a light that doesn't disturb the eyes but is sufficiently bright (so that faces are bright, and signs are bright and legible!). It's pleasant to walk. The twinkling corridors become broader, and all of a sudden there's a real street. The walls of the buildings along the street have drawings scrawled everywhere, a kind of continuous fresco that jumps from wall to wall. There are some adolescent graffiti, of course. Teenagers are the same everywhere and take pleasure in testing themselves in that borderland between speech and obscenity. And then all traces of their work are wiped away and something else is drawn in its place—it's the struggle for space... While this reflection is taking place (semi-delirious, though based on observed reality), the nurse gives Klyucharyov a shot.

A doctor and nurse are taking care of Klyucharyov. He is lying there with the soft light from the ceiling in his eyes. Oh yes, the lighting here is a wonder. The joyous (the only word for it) reflection on the walls, the beautiful bright calendars, and even their white medical coats take in (above and beyond obligatory cleanliness) particles of this diffused warm light. Klyucharyov knows that he's in a small clinic that administers first aid. Yet there's no feeling of frightening sterility here. The examining table itself is like an ottoman—make yourself comfortable. And when Klyucharyov leaves, say, in half an hour or however long it will take, the light will not be altered—it will move on, as it were, along with Klyucharyov, now transformed into the soft light in the halls and the never-waning light of the streetlamps and then over the tables in the wine cellar where Severyanych and Tanya Yeremeyeva have remained, and where the light will merge into a mild and cozy wash of yellow that is in complete harmony with the warm cream-colored tablecloths...

Meanwhile the doctor is speaking: "The wound was beginning to heal. But you obviously ripped it open again. And you've been in shock from the pain. You haven't lost much blood, though, so you won't have to be hospitalized for long."

They examine him with the same respect as one would examine, say, a famous athlete. Probably that's their style. And they're exaggerating, of course. But Klyucharyov has already noted something a bit artificial about their concern. He speaks calmly, though he makes himself understood: "What do you mean hospitalized, Doctor? I can't stay."

The nurse has opened the ampules he needs.

Finally, the doctor taps still another ampule, a red one, with his finger. He names the drug and gives his instructions:

"Three shots in the shoulder. There's something wrong with the ligaments there. Some old injury perhaps." (Was he carrying something heavy?...)

While remembering that he still hadn't made his purchases, Klyucharyov once again thinks about the clever lighting here: the lamps in front of the stores are amazing—bright, yet not too bright to obscure the flickering neon signs. In addition, from somewhere inside spotlights cast beams of light like sword blows onto some item so that you can see perfectly what's displayed—the items don't reflect the light, they absorb it (and as a result they appear larger and more imposing).

These incessant thoughts about light probably are some kind of after-shock delirium. (The first thing that Klyucharyov saw when he opened his eyes was the nurse holding the ampules. They reflected the light from the lamps and glistened like little stars.)

The nurse gives shot after shot while the doctor, who's sitting on a stool opposite Klyucharyov, discusses the case: "You're lucky you fell nearby. You did fall, didn't you?... And did you lose consciousness earlier? No?... Then it was a traumatic shock. But overall it's nothing serious. I won't alarm you further..." And now he asks all of a sudden, without changing the tone of the conversation, as if it's the most natural thing, "*So, how are things up there now?*" Klyucharyov answers: "The same as before." "Of course, of course," says the doctor. (Accept the violence as some kind of test.) "You can get up now," he tells Klyucharyov. Klyucharyov stands up. He sees himself in the reflection of the glass cabinet where the sterile linen and gauze are kept. He sees himself from the side, and as always, the dressed wound seems worse than it actually is. That's to the eye. But he feels fine. He stamps his feet emphatically. He waves his arms. His shoulder hurts a little. "No, no... It's something with your ligaments that's wrong. Something old," the doctor says.

Klyucharyov gets dressed. He expresses his thanks and grabs his shirt, his ski cap with the pompon (the badge of a cultured man), and his sweater from the back of the chair. The bandage sticks to his chest and doesn't bother him at all. The doctor is talking about how important the bandaging is and how ably nurse Tanya dresses wounds, she had done everything essential even before the doctor arrived, such a smart girl. "Say something nice to her, too, on the way out."

As Klyucharyov leaves the clinic, he can feel the four spots on his body where they'd put the iodine and adhesive. He'd get used to it soon, they said. But even so he doesn't feel the bandage itself when he moves.

Now he'd like a shot of vodka.

A SHOT OF VODKA. He enters a place where people are standing and drinking—if people are standing, it'll be fast. He sees the vending machine—ah yes, half a ruble! The small glass is already there. Waiting. And even in this tiny drinking spot the lights are soft and so cleverly concealed. There's light everywhere and you can't tell where it's coming from. Klyucharyov throws the coin into the slot of the machine, keeping his eye fixed on his money so that it doesn't slip out, and... only now does he notice the tiny light! Its light is reflected for a moment on the silver edge of the half-ruble coin—so that's where it comes from! With the smile of one in the know, Klyucharyov leans very slightly over the change counter, takes a look—yes, the bulb is there. They've positioned it so well! How clever. It was only discovered by the half-ruble, like a third eye—and rightly so, since the eye doesn't like its retina to be irritated by light. And maybe light doesn't like to irritate the eye. Reciprocity. Klyucharyov drinks down his vodka in two gulps and leaves, feeling at once the intoxicating liquid and the rapid awakening of his body.

THE SHOVEL. Klyucharyov isn't embarrassed by the missing buttons on his shirt—his sweater covers it. In general he's in a good mood. As for his appearance, he's more worried about the belt on his pants; it's becoming more worn each time he goes through the narrow gap and then pushes his way back up. Klyucharyov is clearly afraid that someday the pants will fall down—perhaps he should buy a belt while he's here? On the corner he sees a good restaurant where people are leisurely eating and drinking. Sitting properly. They know how. Ah, there are some small stores and kiosks just past the restaurant–that's what he needs. The newspaper store is open. And there are candies and drinks too. There are plenty of these little stores and they're all open, but Klyucharyov isn't in a hurry to buy anything here. His belt is holding for the time being, so Klyucharyov turns left again and walks toward the warehouses. It's true that warehouses are stores too, but there are almost no shoppers here, people are walking past. And as a matter of fact, why should they be in a hurry to get tools?

But here you can acquire (or for a small sum simply rent) any and every kind of tool. You can even drive off on some little tractor, but what would Klyucharyov do with it? (No, he needs a shovel.) The warehouse is an extended one-story shed with five storage doors; Klyucharyov notices a woman with a bunch of keys near the first door–she's the one in charge. Warehouses are run the same way everywhere in the world: I'll issue it if I want to; if I don't, I won't. Saint Peter at the heavenly gates. (The lady is getting on in years.) Of course, she'll give Klyucharyov a shovel if he asks nicely, but, of course, she won't feel like it.

She holds the key chain up at eye level and jingles the keys.

"Oh no, my friend. It's already evening..."

"And what a marvelous evening, Lyalya!" Klyucharyov goes on the attack after remembering her name.

But it turns out he hasn't remembered too well–she's not Lyalya. There's nothing to do now but press on, and Klyucharyov quickly becomes jubilant and explains to her that she is Lyalya all the same, and there can be no mistake here because Lyalya is a name for every tender-hearted woman, every kind woman capable of being affectionate and capable of understanding a man (and issuing him a shovel without demanding a large fee).

"Is that so?... Really?" She's flirting. She licks her lips, primps, and smooths out her official violet smock. (His lengthy oratory doesn't matter very much, what matters a great deal is her inner state.) And lo and behold. Looking straight into Klyucharyov's eyes, she's already saying, "I had myself a real drink today. Brandy. And then wine..."

And she looks at him. "Lya-llya-llya-lya," she hums in a voice that is unsteady but not phony.

"I need a shovel."

"A shovel, I'll give you a shovel. Lya-llya-llya..."

He would have to play along and please her. A bit uncomfortable, Klyucharyov sizes things up out of the corner of his eye—she's old but still plump in places. She's still a woman. Probably he'll manage. And having made up his mind, he gives her a bold wink—hey, you're really something!

She has just brought out a shovel. And a small crowbar. Moreover, it seems she wants Klyucharyov to keep on seeking her favor. (Otherwise the sugar won't be sweet.)

"And a pickax," he requests.

Narrowing her eyes and every other minute humphing: "Get a load of that!... So you don't have picks either. How do you paupers live up there?" she brings out a pickax too. She locks the door. And Klyucharyov has only a fleeting glimpse of the storeroom which is so beautiful and so austere inside. Rows of tools wrapped in plastic. Order. Rows and pyramids. Thousands of cans of paint. But she's already locking her door, looking after her workplace. Klyucharyov puts his arm around her and leads her down the hall, passing other doors while taking a look around: "Say, where is there a quiet little room around here with some sacks of something? But no coal sacks, right?..." He has guessed exactly how to talk to her, and she answers with a pleased laugh: "You've got nerve, you!" And suddenly she's trying to free herself—is she held in a firm grip? She jerks away for a moment, yields at once, and from then on moves in step with him, their bodies in tune. They make their way to the very end of the warehouse and go in the last door. Sure enough, there are sacks. Klyucharyov performs his function quickly and rather roughly, but even so she seems quite content. "It's too bad you're in a hurry..." she complains a little. "You didn't get to know me," she says after a pause, meaning that she could show more of herself as a woman, reveal herself in the course of love, but not the first time. She liked to keep company with men, she said, and loved to play cards, she'd been playing poker recently. Yes, she'd learned. A fat guy with a mustache had taught everyone at the warehouse. "You didn't get to know me," she repeats. She's the boss here and Klyucharyov doesn't argue. "That can be corrected, Lyalya, life is long," Klyucharyov assures her; "and there's no point in our hurrying," he says. But despite his words, he gets up immediately and straightens himself up with a great deal of energy.

"I'll rest a while," she says. Or is it he, Klyucharyov, who quietly asks "will you rest a while?" and does she only nod in reply?

She continues to lie on the sacks in her clean violet smock. The sacks are elastic, the laziness heavenly. She lies and listens in quiet to herself, to her relaxed, well-tended body. She no longer looks at Klyucharyov. He's no longer needed. She looks at the ceiling. (While Klyucharyov stands at the door, worrying about how he's going to carry the shovel, crowbar and pickax he has collected.) Her body feels pleasant to the touch and isn't disturbed in the least, and if she did cry out at the moment, it was not from passion, but only because Klyucharyov had unintentionally hurt her when his arms had pressed in on her bones. "No, don't, don't press so hard, spare my flesh."

Klyucharyov leaves. "Goodbye, Lyalya."

"Leave the door open a little." She continues to lie and look at the ceiling and at an old unraveled Gobelin which portrays a medieval battle–a jumble of knights' bodies and horses. In an intimate moment Klyucharyov, half-turning, had suddenly seen a knight blowing a horn, but later he lost him. Klyucharyov is loaded down with his equipment and he gives the cloth a quick glance, lowering his eyes all the way down to the sacks and their beautiful seals and the enormous letters on their sides: KUZMIN and LYUMBKE.

NO SMOKING. KUZMIN and LYUMBKE. Knights and monks. The Gobelin is that old. Galloping horses. Fallen horses with hooves flung in the air. But Klyucharyov doesn't see the horn-blower.

And everywhere there are people, lots of people. Shiny cars crawl carefully down the street. A young couple is walking toward Klyucharyov, a slightly tipsy woman who's laughing and a drunken young man; they are both beautiful, both are carrying ice-cream, and Klyucharyov has to stop and wait with the equipment he's trying to balance (How else can he do it? Maybe put the shovel and crowbar over his shoulder?), because the smiling and completely oblivious pair is headed straight at him. Behind them is a group of people no longer young, friends who have come to meet each other here—the stages of life. They walk in a tight bunch. A trio of hired gypsies is with them—violin, guitar, and accordion. The gypsy with the violin jumps several steps ahead...

He could have stopped to listen for a while, but Klyucharyov is in a hurry. He enters the pub through a side door so that he can get to the back rooms right away. Klyucharyov quickly moves past the small tables along the black-and-white checkerboard floor without stopping, and as he's walking, he raises his eyes to look—there's the hatch. The jagged opening is visible against the white ceiling and is narrowing and turning darker. (Severyanych, Tanya Yeremeyeva, and the aging Ivan Nikolayevich, who in the meantime had joined them, are sitting at their table but they don't see Klyucharyov. Their faces are happy. Klyucharyov is not going to take leave of them, say goodbye—there's no time. Next time he'll sit with them a while longer.)

Klyucharyov is right in the corner now. With a gentle push, he rolls out a specially adjusted and rather light ladder, then climbs up it to the hatch. The ladder resembles the boarding stairs of an airplane—it also moves on small wheels and is just about as steep, but when you reach the top, instead of an airplane hatch (from which departing presidents, hats off, ordinarily wave to us), instead of that hatch there's a jagged black hole in the earth.

THE HOLE HAS BECOME NARROWER. Klyucharyov crawls forward, holding on tightly, and squeezes his way into the neck of the hole. In the narrow part he can relax a little, since the force of friction holds him against the earth. After he has a good grip, he raises the shovel in his right hand–in other words, pushes it over his head–and then with a twist of his hand he throws the shovel up and out, noting the slight rasping sound of its fall. Now he climbs back down to the top rung of the ladder and picks up the crowbar–fortunately, it's light–and after he has squeezed into the narrow neck and wedged himself there, he repeats the same process with the crowbar, though with more precaution (after swinging it back he flings it out with great force and then immediately shields the top of his head with his arm–if the throw is bad, the crowbar could kill him as it falls back down). The crowbar catches the edge of the earth as it swings out, and gravel and sand pour down with a whoosh on top of his head. If he were to throw the pickax up, of course, it would stick in the earth–it can't be done. And his arm is tired.

Klyucharyov is disturbed by the pickax fastened to his stomach, but the worst problem is the neck–the gap has narrowed. This might be a sign that it's close to the river–the natural washing away of a steep bank over the years (and over centuries) causes shifts in the ground that are greater than those created by erosion. Or had some tectonic changes created an instability in the earth's interior which had then affected the surface as well?... It's always an electrifying experience. He, Klyucharyov, knows only that something is happening to the earth all the time (every hour even). The earth breathes; we are jolted by processes whose nature we don't understand; it's clear that we can't sit things out somewhere in quiet; and although there are scientific explanations and hypotheses, to be sure, nature nonetheless remains nature–a mystery. The hole is narrowing, that's all that can be said;

it's being squeezed in, its edges are giving way—the whole simplicity of the earth's behavior consists in this. And sometimes a hole grows wider. (That also happens. There's simplicity in this too.)

The pickax, which has been pressing against Klyucharyov, deforms his body even more as he pushes his way through; since it is fastened to his stomach, it's pulled forward with Klyucharyov, and the sharp points of the two hewing edges scrape and engrave furrows on the rounded stony walls of the hole. They adapt to each other—the pickax and his stomach—and yet Klyucharyov is squeezed so tightly that he thinks about retreat, he considers turning back. (He could always crawl out and then pull up the pickax with a rope—but there isn't any rope, of course; the warehouse flashes in his mind, for a moment he sees old Lyalya's plump flesh—if he has to, he'll manage without the pick. Breathing is hard now and Klyucharyov begins to gasp for air with his mouth open; the air is damp and sandy.) Klyucharyov's shoulders are scraped as they squeeze in and push forward, bearing the weight of the jerking and wiggling that is essential for him to crawl ahead. A worm moves this way, and people move this way, too, if they're in tune with nature. Does it hurt? Of course, it hurts. Klyucharyov's right hand is extended the whole time—he's like a swimmer on his side, and his left hand is at his stomach, trying to protect himself from the pain caused by the pickax, which makes sudden thrusts into his ribs. That's when it really hurts. Klyucharyov writhes, his face and his eyes filling up with dark sand. His left hand searches for the edges of the pickax at the same time as his body makes another attempt to push its way forward. It's hard because the pickax is stuck. Again his left hand gropes around, fumbles, tries to pull the pickax up against his body to where it had been before. Groaning, and in pain, Klyucharyov jerks (just pulling doesn't work) the pickax higher and higher and, with some room to spare even, he guides it over the soft part of his stomach—the scrap of bandage that fastened the pick to his belt had slipped a long time ago and probably was crumpled into a small wad. Inch by inch the pickax passes over Klyucharyov, the sharp points are now at the level of his chest, at his nipples, though off to the sides. The pick bothers Klyucharyov even more now, but he's not afraid of losing it. He manages to squeeze his shoulders in a little more so that he can crawl on further, but the points weigh upon him, they dig into his forearms–but he still must keep on crawling. Klyucharyov begins to shake, he almost cuts his right arm open on the pickax. He tries to reason: be calm. You're already in the narrowest part, in the neck itself–and the further you go, the easier it will be. He forces himself to breathe more rhythmically, and at the same time he catches the first smell of fresh air, air from *outside.* The uncontrollable convulsive shaking ceases at last. He calms himself. Now Klyucharyov frees his shoulder; to be more precise, he shoves his right shoulder up and out of the range of the pickax's edges, moves it as much as he can, and only then does his left shoulder come into use, mimicking the tactics of worms crawling through obstructions, something that everyone knows intuitively if, to repeat, he is not out of tune with nature. Klyucharyov moves on a bit (ten centimeters? fifteen?), scraping off more skin, but as a reward his shoulders are able to rise and fall again without the sharp pain, and by precisely this means (the right one pushing up, the left one pulling down and then making an adjustment), by repeating this maneuver many times, Klyucharyov now moves up to a height at which the black earth breathes in his face: his eyes still cannot see the soil, but he can already feel the breathing of that thin dark layer that nourishes every living thing. Everything's easier. He can shake the sand off his head. Just a bit more. Without thinking–yet this happens completely consciously–Klyucharyov suddenly tears the pickax from his body and flings it outward, almost hitting the outside with his hand as he throws it, since the edge is right there. The edge of the earth, if you're coming from the inside. While tossing his head to shake the sand and earth out of his hair, he catches a glimpse of the bright sky. But this is a common illusion when one looks up at the sky from a hole. Just one more push with his arms—and Klyucharyov climbs out. It's the same evening. It's getting dark.

He staggers from weakness. He has collapsed on the ground, into the green of the grass. The shovel and the crowbar lie next to him and farther on is the pickax that he threw out with his last strength. He recovers his breath. Slowly. A spasm of release. If he looks ahead, he can see their five-story apartment house, built back in Khrushchev's time. In the dusk the buildings are completely distinguishable, and his house, which juts out a little, is visible too. If he looks to the left, he'll see the shimmers of light on the lead-colored river.

THE IDEA HE DOES NOT BELIEVE IN ALL THAT MUCH is the idea of the cave. (Which has to be close enough to his home, the five-story building.) Klyucharyov tries to pick out a place. He backs up and takes a few steps down. The ravine slopes to the river—that's convenient. A ravine is a kind of cut itself, and it's easier to dig here, for the principle of every cave is simple and requires you to dig from the side and not straight in. It's easier to thrust in the shovel and the removal is simple because the soil is flung or scatters down on its own; it doesn't pile up in molehills and won't bother a stranger's eye. Yes, on a slight slope. But not too far down. So that it doesn't flood when water streams downhill.

Klyucharyov looks around for a minute: he's memorizing the surroundings. Tall weeds. Two gnarled birches whose bowed branches trail over the ground, and above them, on the slope, a very mature bird-cherry tree. And to imprint it fully in his memory—those slightly dry nettles at the edge of the ravine.

After he marks out a little path in his mind, visible only to him, Klyucharyov pushes aside some weeds. Here. The shovel and the crowbar are put aside for now; in their place the pickax goes straight to work and most effectively. It wasn't for nothing that he'd crawled the entire way through the hole with it, almost driving it into his collarbone when he was crushed. He digs. The idea Klyucharyov does not believe in all that much is his minimum program: if he's not able to team up with anyone, Klyucharyov will be able to dig out a cave for himself and his family in the event it becomes impossible to live in apartments. He digs.

He throws off his sweater, but doesn't want to stop and risk losing his initial energy. Now (still not stopping) he grabs the shovel. The loosened earth flies down in lumps and bits, and then Klyucharyov evens out the hollow space he'd first broken open with the rough pickax. Carefully smoothing out and trimming the edges with his shovel, Klyucharyov notices that so far the result just reminds him of a burrow or maybe of the hole he had crawled through, which he'd worked his way through just a moment ago with such pain and difficulty—yes, he was copying it unconsciously. What can one do, it's not intuitive so much as subintuitive, *terrestrial* thinking, which adopts the experience of the other without having even admitted it to consciousness—that is what is guiding him. The track of centuries. The motion of crawling and the testing of scraped (smoothed) shoulders and knees, assimilated through distant contact with the experience of millenia, of those millenia when the experience of the other or the experience of one's own self had not yet occurred and there was only one kind of experience—the present one. Klyucharyov is tired. The bandage, which cuts into his chest, and the adhesive are irritating his skin again. While he was pushing through the gap, he didn't feel the bandage, but after swinging the pickax for a while, his body breaks out in sweat. Good. Now he can fit into the cave up to his waist. Suddenly he hears sounds. Ah! Below there's a brook rippling softly, which means that somewhere very near, fresh spring water is running to the river, water with a source right here in the ravine. That's very convenient. He won't have to run back and forth to the river. (It might not be safe right by the river, just like in the apartments. Or in every open place.)

Klyucharyov hides the tool in the bushes. He'll come back a little later and dig some more, it's not night yet.

He must call Chursin. (He has to try and call.) And Olya Pavlova, of course.

But how can you make a call from a street devoid of life?... There aren't any receivers in the phone booths; they've been ripped out and thrown away. A piece of wire sticks out and that's all. Klyucharyov walks further. He must try. In the next telephone booth down the street the telephone receiver had also been ripped out, but at least it's visible—the receiver lies at his feet, crushed by a few kicks from a boot. All that's missing is the cloud of dust. The flattened telephone receiver is impressive and puts your imagination to work (forcing you to picture a giant ear).

There's not a soul. A single pedestrian had stepped out, but when he caught sight of another person, he darted behind the corner of a building and waited there. (Waited for Klyucharyov to pass.) The windows in the buildings are dark. Certainly there are people living in some apartments, but they've barricaded themselves in and covered the windows with the thickest possible curtains in order to keep the light in the window from giving them away. Curtains are our padlocks. We're not here. No one is here. We don't exist *at all.*

Keeping the same pace, Klyucharyov walks past a store that's been locked up. He walks past a broken display window. (But manages to look back: someone has jumped out from behind a building.)

"Wait!" Klyucharyov cries out hurriedly.

The man disappears quickly.

"Wait a minute! I'm not going to chase you!" Klyucharyov cries out louder.

Klyucharyov's voice sounds surprisingly resonant in the empty street, it booms out (Klyucharyov's surprised too), and the man quickens his pace even more, breaking into a run and tucking his head down between his shoulders, as if after the shouting Klyucharyov would probably take aim at him.

There's no one to ask. Klyucharyov is alone in the middle of the street—at last in the distance (the farsightedness of a forty-seven-year-old bookworm) he makes out a pay phone with a receiver hanging in good condition in the right place; he heads there, hurries over! But, needless to say, this telephone is defective too. Frequent beeps are spouted in his ear without end; having expressed all their anger to others over this phone, people have hung up for good.

Klyucharyov still hasn't torn the receiver from his ear, but somehow he has the sense to notice a squeak in between beeps—it's the squeaking of a door. He looks around. Behind the telephone booth he can see the entrance to an apartment building. The door is wide open, but since it's also firmly secured, it means this isn't the door that's squeaking, it's a door inside. He walks into the entrance. There it is. One of the apartments on the first floor is open and a slight draft pushes the door back and forth. The apartment doesn't seem to have been looted yet. Was that a voice?... No, the television is on. As usual, the announcer reports facts confirming the gradual normalization of conditions.

Everything's in place. The apartment is deserted. The watermarks of absence. Just in case, Klyucharyov walks through the rooms without turning on a light. There's a telephone.

A miracle—splendid rings, few and far between. He can call.

Olya Pavlova bursts into tears and confirms that Pavlov has died. He died on the street from a heart attack, there are still no details. Olya sobs and chokes on her tears. Maybe he'd had a chance scuffle with someone? A fight?... No. She doesn't know.

"How are the Chursins?"

"No news..." Olya Pavlova says she constantly calls the Chursins; she hears intermittent rings, the telephone is working, but no one comes to the phone.

Olya cries. She tells how they didn't know what to do with Pavlov's body, and as a result right now his body is still lying in the Third Medical Institute and it's horrible for her—it's awful and horrible to think that students will soon be training and doing their experiments on him, on his dead body, just like on any of the unclaimed dead. "What sort of training! What students!" Klyucharyov yells, trying to calm her down. "You've lost your mind! Who needs a corpse now?!" It is appalling to use that expression with respect to the dead Pavlov, but Klyucharyov isn't able to correct himself. He's in a hurry. He's in a hurry to dispel her alarm—the problem is that Olya Pavlova is pregnant. She is in her fifth or sixth month. And he must deflect her anxiety, even with a forceful and convincing outburst if necessary.

Klyucharyov is shouting at her (and for her), but he's not so confident himself. The electricity in the city is shut off evenings and nights, but it's still possible that in the morning work will go on at the Institute.

"Don't cry! Don't cry, Olya!" Klyucharyov says that he'll come, he'll help bury him. He promises, he swears he'll come. "Don't cry!"

After Olya Pavlova he calls the Chursins, but no one picks up the phone. Klyucharyov remembers that the Chursins have an ancient dacha and he also remembers the phone number. He calls there too, but without success.

Death always comes at a bad time. (Although, in essence, it is the most natural thing in a person's life. All told, it's simply the end of life.) But, God knows, Klyucharyov has so little desire to go off somewhere right now, in these difficult times, to bury poor Pavlov; he just doesn't want to have all the bother, make all the effort, do so much talking, and especially in the presence of the mourning Olya Pavlova, who has no idea how to get anything done in general and less so now that she's pregnant. He thinks about the secondary importance of death. Of course, Klyucharyov will go. Of course, his feeling of duty toward the dead man will stir and give Klyucharyov a good kick in the pants, it will give him a push and get him going, but that moment hasn't come yet and at this moment he, Klyucharyov, isn't ready, he's even dismayed by what a nuisance this is just now, how inconvenient.

Who else should I call, he thinks. (Since there's a telephone right there that's not disconnected. But he can't remember any more numbers.) Klyucharyov leaves the apartment. He pretends to close the door, but leaves it slightly ajar by squeezing a small tightly-folded piece of newspaper between the door and the metal strip of the lock. (The door's open, but no one besides Klyucharyov will notice it. He'll come back to make phone calls. Life isn't over.)

And then it suddenly hits him—the door had been left open on purpose *for others, for everyone;* after all, he had made his phone call only because the door was open and it was squeaking besides. Needless to say, Klyucharyov also leaves the door open. (Let it squeak.) He'll just remember the number of the building and entrance.

2

AT HOME. When Klyucharyov arrives home, his wife is feeding their son. Their son is an enormous fourteen-year-old who contracted an illness as a child and is now slowly catching up in his development. He has poor control of his hands, especially the small muscle movements (he isn't able to fasten buttons) and he speaks poorly (as if his mouth were full of kasha)—but with the hope that his mental condition can be improved; it's not impossible, there is hope, but time drags on so slowly in such situations! In the meantime the son has become huge, he's like a five-year-old child with gentle eyes who's a whole head taller than Klyucharyov and significantly stronger and sturdier in the upper body. In size and weight he exceeds Klyucharyov's wife, that is, his own mother, by about four times.

"Keep it up, keep it up!" As soon as he enters, Klyucharyov's voice encourages their important activity.

"We're doing a good job," his wife replies; she and their son are both holding on to one enormous spoon. The son is bringing the spoon toward his mouth by himself, but he needs an extra little push, so his mother's hand grasps the spoon as its trajectory falls short, adding the necessary bit of force, and the spoon of mashed potato lands between his sluggishly chewing jaws.

"Ahn-na-nuff neat," he utters. (I've had enough to eat.)

But his mother guides his hand again, and again he obediently scoops something up and again obediently eats it, just as children who are delayed in their development always do.

She tells Klyucharyov, "We have to get in touch with the Chursins in spite of everything. And with the Pavlovs..."

"Yes."

"We've just completely lost track of each other!" She continues to feed their son.

Her fear that the Klyucharyovs will be isolated makes it easier for him to leave soon. (He takes note of this.) But he doesn't hurry. The comforts of home.

He doesn't tell his wife about Pavlov's death and the need to bury him; instead he quickly tells her that he has found a place not far from their building and the river and he has already started to dig the shelter. They had talked about it earlier, but now his wife is asking more forcefully, she needs to be convinced. Would it really be more terrible to stay in the building? Why?... Klyucharyov explains. It all depends on the circumstances, imagine there's no water, no light, and, of course, the toilets and sewer system don't work–our home is no longer a home. And if half of the apartment building is empty besides and strangers come there to sleep and to smoke and settle scores, then at three or four o'clock in the morning their wonderful fifth-floor apartment is certain to go up in flames and it will burn for quite a long time because the fire truck (even if it comes) won't find a place to pump water from. As for the cave, it's splendid, he has already dug it out up to his waist. He'll dig deeper, chop some branches, line the inside–they'll think of something to cover it with from the outside. And when they move there they'll take warm things...

Klyucharyov cheerfully continues talking–his intonation affects hers. In the meantime he goes into the bathroom, takes off his shirt, moistens a wad of cotton with iodine, and in the same apparent spirit of inexhaustible cheer, rubs the scratches and the edges of his wound with the cotton so that they won't become inflamed. His wife has finished the feeding. She puts the teakettle on the hotplate. Then she goes and stands behind Klyucharyov and with another ball of cotton—dab, dab, dab—she works on his back, which he can't reach with his own hand. She lifts up the bandage and swabs beneath it. As if she's putting stamps on a large envelope.

"I can tell from your cuts that the hole has gotten even narrower—what's happening to it?"

"Ask what's happening to the earth, instead... It's the earth that's contracting, not the hole."

His wife doesn't want to get into an argument. She works on his back. Raising up one of his trouser legs, she says "Check your legs!"

But Klyucharyov's legs are tough—they don't have any cuts on them, and he's not concerned about the inflamed abrasions.

Klyucharyov remains cheerful, the tone he has adopted keeps him from blurting out anything about Pavlov. Yes, of course, he'll be leaving in a minute—off to the Pavlovs and then the Chursins. Yes, of course, friends are friends, it's important to keep in contact. But he'll need to hurry, it will start to get dark soon. Yes, it's evening, his wife nods in agreement.

They wash their son. After they undress him, it becomes even more obvious how large he is. He stands in the bath like an immense white mountain and sobs very quietly—he's afraid of the water. The water gurgles as it runs and runs. (It's good they have it.) After they've finished the difficult and painstaking job of moving their son into the bath, Klyucharyov sits down on the edge of the tub and for a while his breathing is strained. His wife picks up the loofah and washes her son's hands. "The right one... And now the left. See what a good job we've done!" Next they begin to persuade the boy to sit down—don't be scared, I'll hold on to your hand—and the water practically flies up from the bottom of the tub; in just a few seconds the tub is completely full, his massive body has taken up so much space that the water rises to the very top. He's no longer shivering, it feels nice. His eyes are filled with gratitude. He's a good child. His backwardness in relation to his peers has not weighed on his inner world; it has even given him a radiance, and it is this glance, these grateful eyes, that Klyucharyov is unable to bear. My child, he thinks. He has turned his face aside, but now the son strokes his father's back with the hand that is held. Maybe their son knows that his voice is wheezy and unclear and because of this doesn't say "Papa...," but at this moment the touch of his palm utters precisely this word and no other. It is perfectly clear.

"Now it's your turn," says Klyucharyov's wife.

She leaves. Klyucharyov washes his son's groin and genitals—we have a fully developed man on our hands, even if he's fourteen, and it's not at all related to the hormones he started taking just a year ago. (The additional body hair is from the drugs.) Klyucharyov carefully soaps up the loofah, then scrubs and washes him inch by inch. A restless man who is getting older, he loves his son; the boy plays gently with an unsinkable rubber lion, making bubbles over and over again. But all of a sudden, with a final gurgle, the lion nevertheless drowns. Then his Denis reaches for a baby duck and the water almost runs over its edge as he shifts in the tub. The boy casts a cautious and sly glance at Klyucharyov, not because of the water that's tossing from his awkward movements, but because Klyucharyov had once explained to him that baby ducks are girls' toys, and the lion, elephant, and boat are toys for him.

"Are we washing his hair today?" Klyucharyov shouts to his wife somewhere in the apartment.

"No..."

He washes the soap off his son's strong back, lets the soapy water out, then rinses him one more time, spraying a clean stream of water from the shower all over his clean body—stand up, my boy. He helps him get up, his son's afraid because it's slippery. "Up you go!" Klyucharyov says, imparting confidence with his voice, while bearing the heaviness on his own chest and shoulder. Denis leans all his enormous weight on him, but while Klyucharyov grunts, his son, good boy, manages to remove his right leg from the bathtub and put it on the floor—there. The first step is hard.

ALONG THE DESERTED STREET—TO BUS NO. 28. What can he do if the rest of the transport system has stopped working, and if only one bus runs in their district. Let's be thankful for that. The bus takes a circuitous, winding route, but at least you can get to other parts of the city and once there, transfer if you're lucky.

Not a soul. Klyucharyov is waiting at the bus stop. Around a bus stop people are usually cursing about the dog excrement that's lying around, saying it's disgraceful no one removes it. The asphalt platform is remarkably clean now. Since the only things left to eat are canned goods and grains, dog lovers have taken their dogs out of the city and let them go, as they put it, with a "you're on your own." Others have gone to the country, to some very distant, dark spot, of course. They've gone if they have a car, that is, and only if they managed to get gas. There isn't any gas. It's futile to try. Cars sit lifelessly by the buildings. They're so useless that the owners don't even look at them from behind their thickly curtained windows.

The bus pulls up—it's empty. Besides Klyucharyov there's just one passenger on the bus, an old woman. The whole time she keeps on telling Klyucharyov some stupid story—probably out of fear. (Despite the fact that Klyucharyov got on through the rear door and took a seat relatively far from her, five rows back.)

Two days ago, the old woman recounts, a group of people got on the bus and took all the shoes that were any good off the women's feet. And the men's shoes too. And everyone gave them up without a murmur and they grabbed all the shoes and got off at the next stop. At least they could have offered people some felt slippers in exchange for their shoes, the way they do in museums, the old woman quips and glances back at Klyucharyov so that he'll say something in reply, preferably something equally witty.

One of those intrepid old women.

"Well, I wouldn't have given up my boots," she laughs quietly.

The bus slows down before a stop, then instead of stopping, it suddenly begins to hum, lets out a roar, takes off, and speeds past. Klyucharyov looks out the window and sees three men who brandish their fists and look threatening to the driver. The driver's decided not to risk it. The bus rushes through the empty streets.

At last the intrepid old woman gets off the bus. Klyucharyov is alone. From the driver he learns that this route intersects with the lines of two operating buses (only two), and now he considers which of the two would best take him out of the city to the Chursins' dacha. The bus flies like a bullet. Buildings with sealed dark windows fill the streets. There's not a single light.

Klyucharyov thinks of his boy's eyes. They're so gentle and good. What's more, if suddenly they briefly convey some understanding of the present situation (How does he feel it? Through what mysterious knowledge?) and an understanding of his own misfortune as well, he'll ask, "Ahn na, naht nong ne?" (Papa, what's wrong with me?) And Klyucharyov falls apart, he's not able to endure that gaze. My boy. He'll never crawl through any kind of hole. And what will happen to his son if Klyucharyov somehow accidentally dies? Once there lived a Sergei Leonidovich Pavlov–and now there's no Sergei Leonidovich Pavlov. My boy has beautiful eyes. They never express anything inessential or commonplace. They contain a knowledge that people are aware of but unable to express. (The knowledge of how sad and unprotected people are.) Klyucharyov usually turns away when he can't endure his son's gaze, but the boy notices. Notices and understands. He is sensitive. He puts his hand on Klyucharyov's shoulder or back, and if he feels his father's inaudible soft shudders, he says, "Na, ahn na, na." (Don't, Papa, don't.)

* * *

Klyucharyov still has to transfer buses twice before he can get to where the dacha is. Movement comes only with the swerves and zigzags of the route—be thankful they're there—and when his travel on wheels comes to an end, Klyucharyov surveys the surroundings and goes on foot in the direction from which he can already smell pine trees and needles. Where the dachas are.

First he passes a massive fence as impenetrable as a wall—a refuge that's certainly safe; no one will ever know if you're living here or not, if you've gone somewhere or are hiding out. The fence is stately and tall and inspires respect. But the stateliness soon stops. Now on both sides there are more ordinary little dachas with small plots of land and picket fences that are pitifully protected by lilacs and can be seen through from far away. At one of these wretched and obviously abandoned dachas he sees a dog dying. Unfed and forgotten, the dog lies by his house without the strength to get up. Compassion for the animal (I still have it! Klyucharyov realizes with amazement) prompts Klyucharyov to go through the gate and untie him from the chain, but it turns out that the dying dog isn't bound. He's just there as usual. And though other starving dogs have run away, something has held this one back, be it love or duty. He looks at Klyucharyov with the serene glance of an animal sensing death. Klyucharyov feels around in his pocket, breaks off half a piece of sugar, and places it nearby.

The Chursins have one of these wretched gray dachas too, and Klyucharyov doubts he would have found it in the approaching darkness had that monotonous landscape not suddenly appeared before his eyes. An ordinary edge of forest. A twist, a bend in the road. A pine tree at the bend. This is Chursin's edge of the wood, a bend in the road that he had more than once pointed out to Klyucharyov and said of it—here's a part of my life. He, Chursin, could look at this bend in the road forever. He even comes in the rain. Klyucharyov has no idea what spirits stir his friend's mind here, what sort of souls from the past. He doesn't know what it gives to Chursin, but to him, Klyucharyov, it gives an immediate orientation in dacha geography. As if he had a map. Klyucharyov is near their dacha within three minutes. They don't have dogs. Klyucharyov rings the faint bell and then goes in, after first slipping his hand in to unlatch the gate, of course.

The dacha is deserted but it hasn't fallen into neglect. Klyucharyov notices that the blocks of birch on which they liked to sit in earlier times are no longer there. And he also sees that the bindweed running along the terrace has been sprinkled with water recently, the soil is damp. Galka, Chursin's wife, must have been watering it. Or their pretty daughters, real beauties at fifteen and seventeen—Galka has absurd fears about them, she's a complete wreck, and Klyucharyov will probably get an extremely good sense of this very soon (Galka won't want to let Chursin go off with him).

After he finds the key under the floorboard, he goes in. No one's there, it's completely quiet. But there's a piece of paper on the table and someone has written on it in large letters: "DO YOU REMEMBER LAST SUMMER..." The words are cut off with ellipsis points, and Klyucharyov instantly focuses his mind and (like clockwork!) immediately remembers that precisely last summer Chursin took him to his neighbor's dacha, led him there as if on a polite social call. Chursin, who once lived in an orphanage, liked to play tricks on the old neighbor, who by now was completely ancient, but who nonetheless had become quite scared of nuclear war—he'd picked a good thing to be scared of!—and was so driven by this fear that he built a bunker (taking advantage of his former connections here). An acclaimed builder, the old man constructed his bunker simply and intelligently. He buried an enormous tank in the ground, then buried another tank next to it. There was water in one and air in the other: live on and breathe your allotted measure! Naturally, they installed a pipe with a faucet in the neighboring tank: have a drink. "We tossed a silver icon frame in the water—holy water can't be bad for your stomach." They had all started laughing sweetly then, the old man, too.

At this moment, inspired by the strange idea that has just surfaced, Klyucharyov quickly makes his way to the neighbor's dacha. He walks in a straight line—through the garden with the raspberry bushes, the way they had gone before and probably the way the Chursins go now. On the way he eats a few berries he picks off the branches.

He finds the entrance. He knocks. The entrance to the bunker is in the midst of a thick overgrown raspberry patch, even more impressive than the one by the fence. It's several steps down into a pit where the dark bare side of a tank sticks out of the ground like the side of a dinosaur buried in the earth. "Greetings!" says Chursin, as he opens the creaking cover. Klyucharyov squeezes in—the cover had been cut directly from the body of the tank and then set on clumsily welded hinges. Strong, all the same. Inside the tank two candles are burning on a small solid table. One of the daughters holds a third candle in her hands.

"Come in, come in!... We're just sitting here and examining the old man's riches out of boredom."

They explain that the old man died and was buried about three months before. And they proved to be extremely slow-witted: for two whole months the Chursins sat in their dilapidated dacha, locking themselves in with every bolt, blocking the rotting front door with a chest of drawers (that's right, my friend, every night—my wife gave the orders, so what could I do!) until they suddenly figured out what to do. Of course! What could be better!... And now for a week already (no, two, two!) the Chursins have lived in the dacha during the day and as soon as dusk falls they watch the evening news and then head through the raspberry bushes—straight here.

"But I called you at the dacha."

"We don't answer the phone. Do any phones in the city still work?..."

"They disconnected ours, but the Pavlovs' phone worked a couple of days longer."

The weak candlelight shines upon the tall stacks of packages of powdered kissel that surround them. On pyramids of evaporated milk and piles of rice and sugar.

"That's the old man for you! A martyr to an idea! Oh, if only we had a kerosene stove too! Or a primus!... Heaven on earth!" Chursin says happily, ecstatically even, and, of course, they not only point out the supplies that have fallen to their lot, they're prepared to share them: "Yes, sure, come straight here. Yes, yes. If something happens, we'll sit here together and withstand the siege!"

Klyucharyov is skeptical: there's no way Denis could crawl in.

"We'll get him through, we'll take him together by the arms and legs and—full speed ahead!"

The Chursins were good people, especially when they were enthusiastic about something. Moreover, they were the extraordinary sort of people who are ready to share even when they are in need themselves. Nevertheless, Klyucharyov realizes that this remarkable tank doesn't have enough air for many people. As for his Denis, maybe they could push him through once with a few scrapes, but a second time or a third time? And how can Denis be squeezed in, if he has to stay on his own for a while? And if everyone runs off, where will he run?... My boy. He'll sit down in that raspberry patch and not move anywhere anymore. He'll be sitting there watching the little leaves.

Galka Chursin asks Klyucharyov about his wife—they are friends: Forbid her to go out on the street, Klyucharyov, it's dangerous, and there isn't anything in the stores now anyway, is there?... At the same time Chursin is enthusiastically drawing Klyucharyov a pail with a lid, he has thought up a way to make one. They need to have one or two covered pails. Something like a watering can, with the spout cut off. More things to worry about—getting a watering can, getting a primus stove. All three (Klyucharyov included) are excited, they're all speaking practically at once. One beautiful daughter listens to them in silence. The other child-beauty stands completely off to the side, still holding the candle, like a madonna. Next to her, illuminated by the flickering light, stand rows of canned evaporated milk.

Klyucharyov is saying, "Yes, worries; but we still have something else to deal with—we have to bury Pavlov."

After he speaks they sit in silence for a long, sad moment. Pavlov was their friend.

Bit by bit, the conversation shifts on its own into the quarrel Klyucharyov had expected all along. It's easy to understand: Galka doesn't want to let her husband go, she doesn't want to let go of her Chursin, such an energetic and resourceful intellectual with his orphan background. Without him she's terrified. (She and her two adolescent daughters can't live without him.) And Pavlov's already dead, it's too late to save him.

"I'm sure they'll bury Pavlov. And they'll certainly tell Olya where he's buried, in such matters arrangements are always made. There are good people everywhere..."

Olya is pregnant. Olya's alone now—is Klyucharyov's argument.

But why? Why, all the more, should she go out on the dark streets now?

"But, Galya! It's possible we need to get Pavlov. He's lying in the morgue of some medical institute. Why do they need a man who was picked up on the street?"

"If they picked him up that means they'll bury him! Those are precisely the places where people work around the clock and under all kinds of circumstances."

They quarrel. Only the daughter is quiet; with one hand supporting her cheek she watches the candles that are burning on the small table. The other daughter with her candle is still at the far end of the tank-room.

Chursin irritably explains to his wife that they need a kerosene stove, they need a thermos, they need to get them, and in order to get them Chursin has to leave the dacha anyway and go into the city.

"We won't survive here even three hours if we aren't equipped with a gas stove or a primus ahead of time," he screams to his wife.

And at the same time he gives Klyucharyov a wink.

Klyucharyov understands. He says goodbye. He apologizes for having brought such a disturbance into their home, and asks Galya to forgive him—that's the way it is these days. Goodbye. He'll pass on her greetings to his wife and Denis. Thank you.

He leaves and Chursin chases after him (he has to see Klyucharyov off!). As soon as they get out of the raspberry patch, Chursin starts reproaching himself: he'd let himself get carried away by the quarrel and had forgotten that it's best not to quarrel with women, you should deceive them and divert their attention a bit. That's right, a little deception and a little diversion.

By the way, smart leaders always act exactly this way with an unruly nation. (Chursin is taking a swipe at the top brass now: in contrast to Klyucharyov, he doesn't believe in leaders, in their assistants or top bureaucrats, or in that entire quivering swarm circling blindly above us.) Not to deceive them so much as divert their attention, that's what you need—in half an hour Chursin will have another talk with his wife and he'll convince her. He'll definitely convince her. Are you sure? Absolutely. So, I'll be free in an hour or two at the latest and we'll meet soon after at Olya Pavlova's.

They walk past dachas; there's not a soul to be seen the entire long way. People are hiding. Chursin points out the dacha of one Veretenin-Voronin; it's already been robbed three times—they took the dishes and even the blankets. The owners had left long ago.

"The common belief is that the ones who stay in their dachas are the first to be robbed. That's what the people think," Chursin reports deferentially. "Look at the metal bolts over there. And there's a lock that weighs about forty pounds, everyone does what he can! And if you go down that lane, you'll see fences covered with barbed wire. Oh yes, fear is the moving force behind reaction. Once, in the middle of the night, it sounded as if people were test-firing an old machine-gun. I'm not kidding! Really! At first I thought I'd hear a Kalashnikov hammer away too, but I listened carefully, and n-n-n-no—a real machine-gun was clattering. There was a simple explanation–one of the dachas here belongs to an employee of the Civil War museum, obviously he'd brought a gun here. Obviously, he'd stolen it. Why not, if this stoker from the boiler room is a dexterous and capable fellow who can repair a Maxim gun without any trouble or expense. If a Maxim can be repaired, it's something you can depend on. Do you know anyone who works in a museum?"

He's joking, but not joking–that's Chursin. He waves his arms while explaining things energetically. That's also how Chursin cheers up his fearful wife and his silent beautiful daughters. He does his best to get a kerosene stove. He nails boards on the fence. Looks after his unprotected dacha, looks after the bunker. (Like Klyucharyov, who just now remembers his cave.)

They separate and Klyucharyov goes along the road that comes out on the bus route. Chursin turns left to go through the woods. He says it's faster for him to return that way.

But Klyucharyov figures out why he has taken the path to the left. That way Chursin will pass by the edge of the forest. And go by the bend in the road where the pine tree is. He'll stand there for a minute and give himself some space.

VENDING MACHINES WITH CARBONATED WATER, just as before. But the first thing Klyucharyov sees on the empty street is a nervous thief in front of a store window. It's natural for a thief to be afraid, but the approaching night must bring a certain general fear, and Klyucharyov is aware of the fact that he and the thief share this feeling, that they are alike. The window is dark (its surface is like the smooth surface of dark water) and the thief stands as if fused with it. The thief can't be seen against it. It looks as if he's trying to make a hole in the window and force his way into the store–Klyucharyov suddenly notices that he has placed a ruler against the glass and is kneeling there trying to cut out a corner of glass with a small stone, probably a synthetic diamond.

With his ruler he looks like an industrious schoolboy. There's a soft crunch. Klyucharyov only guessed he was a thief when he was a step away from him and now the thief has grabbed the ruler, darted from his place, and hidden behind the corner. A night thief's fright?... Klyucharyov hears the retreating steps, they sound so fragile—it's as though the thief were running away on very thin little legs, and Klyucharyov understands with sudden clarity, connecting everything, that both he and the thief, both of them are afraid of the mob. They have caught this disease. His hearing darts ahead (with prescience), and Klyucharyov catches the not yet existent tread of thousands of feet on the street—*shrakh-shrakh-shrakh!...*

It's getting dark. Not a single car or bus is on the street and, of course, there aren't any people. Klyucharyov cuts straight across the deserted street. There aren't any rules for crossing—he goes this way in order to make a sharper and quicker turn into a side street, and it's right at the corner that he stumbles across the vending machines with the carbonated water. Klyucharyov hits himself painfully on the edge of one. (The only streetlight burning is a bit too far away, by the entrance to the underground crossing.) He gives himself quite a bang. And then it hits. A wave of familiar (though still unswallowed) water strikes the roof of his mouth. Saliva burns his palate, throat, and soul. His eyes water. This forgotten pleasure prompts Klyucharyov to search his pocket for a coin. He has it. He throws it in the slot. It doesn't work. The next machine doesn't work either. But Klyucharyov persists and throws a coin in again. Nothing. Nothing... but now it begins to sputter—look, it's working. And since there aren't any glasses, naturally, Klyucharyov hastily cups his hands together, captures the long-awaited bubbling liquid, and bends down to take a drink. And when the water is gone (so soon!) he wipes his face with his wet palms.

* * *

When a street is deserted as far as the horizon, you notice a person right away, especially if there are several of them. On the other side of Stroitelnaya Street, not on the sidewalk, but somewhat further back, between two buildings, Klyucharyov sees three men raping a woman, they've forced her to her knees. Two of them are holding her, one on each side. A third stands directly in front of her, he has undone his pants and is clumsily jabbing himself in her face and in her mouth. It's all without noise, performed as if in a silent movie, in a kind of slow motion that seems completely natural in this soundless twilight.

Klyucharyov doesn't have any heroic desire to charge across the street, nor any desire to be stabbed between the ribs with a knife for coming to her aid because in a certain sense this twilight is their hour, their time. However, the instinct (or is it a conscious feeling?) to not let them kill her does work at least. Klyucharyov crosses the street and as he gets close to them cries out: "Hey, you bastards!" Klyucharyov's voice is threatening, but he moves toward them slowly, needless to say. Just to scare them off. The experience with the thief at the store is still fresh. "Hey! Bastards!" the roar of his second cry does something, for now they glance up and around, let her loose, and hide. Two of them run off, and then the third. Klyucharyov walks over to her. She has gotten up by now and is leaving, she's young. Klyucharyov walks beside her and scolds her: she can't go out on the street at this hour, he says, doesn't she know that? A middle-aged man in a cap with a pompon–though to be honest, he'd already lost the cap. "It's okay," she says hoarsely, "it's okay."

She's young. They're going the same way along this empty street. After she clears her throat, she tells Klyucharyov in a naive and unexpectedly melodious voice, "A sadist. He wouldn't come no matter what. It was on purpose. He wanted me to choke on it." And here she adds, as if not wanting to blame people unnecessarily, "But the other two were okay. Regular guys."

She complains to him about how terrible it is when there are no movies, nothing to do. That's right, it's no golden age, Klyucharyov agrees. When they reach the corner where Stroitelnaya Street crosses Zhebrunyov, where there's a traffic light which is flashing and changing colors for no apparent reason, Klyucharyov has to make a turn. They both come to a stop before separating. "If it's in a nice way, regular, I'll swallow it... You want to?" she asks. Klyucharyov says he's in a hurry and feels around his head for the cap with the pompon.

"I'm in a hurry too. There's no bus, I've had to walk three or four kilometers already."

She's holding up well. Youth. Before parting, Klyucharyov says that she doesn't seem to be afraid of the streets. "But I'm afraid that suddenly people will start rushing out. Running and trampling. I imagine thousands and thousands of them running along the streets..." She's also afraid of the mob.

THE BUS ROUTES ZIGZAG. But you don't notice it, you don't feel the extra kilometers of distance, and they're not any burden since you're sitting in the bus and, if the bus lights are all on during the ride, it's bright inside the car. It's not night yet, you can still see everything. But maybe the driver feels braver with the lights on.

Klyucharyov's alone in the bus.

But in the next bus Klyucharyov transfers to there's a shy married couple in his car. Klyucharyov listens as they whisper to each other and hears her all at once utter the word "Police..." while showing her husband something outside the window and instilling a little bit of calm in him (or in herself) with her voice. Klyucharyov sees them also—two policemen standing on the empty street. Both with clubs. Both with guns in holsters, which in accordance with the rules of the day aren't hanging at the hip but directly over the stomach, beneath the hand. Of course, one sentry has a two-way radio.

The bus route makes such zigzags that Klyucharyov decides not to take this uncertain route to Olga Pavlova's (with such zigzags you might end up in a completely different part of the city), so first he'll return along a route he knows to the part where his building is. And from there he'll start all over and feel his way along.

As Klyucharyov walks by the river, near the place where he'd started to dig out the cave, he is startled by strange noises. He would have just walked by, but he had found this good hiding place himself. There's nothing for Klyucharyov to hear now (the strange noises have stopped), but he senses something like an abrupt flash behind the two gnarled birches. Right over there. His concern about the cave (and the tools) immediately pushes him on and into battle. "Who's there?" Klyucharyov asks in a threatening voice. The courage of a man in a cap with a little pompon. He directs his voice down the slope, into the ravine, and from there comes a sigh and a voice that is so familiar to Klyucharyov, "Viktor? Is it you?... My God, I was so scared,"–her voice.

HIS WIFE. The flashlight flashes again as Klyucharyov descends to the bird-cherry trees and the gnarled birches—it's the flashlight they use at home. Klyucharyov's wife had fastened it to the branch of a bush and in the ghostly light (the battery barely works) she has decided on her own to continue her husband's work. She has been digging.

"Denis is sleeping," she says, by way of explanation, and so that Klyucharyov won't yell at her she assures him she'd left the house for only five minutes and at this very moment (right now! I swear!) she was getting ready to return home. Her nerves are on edge. To keep from having a fit and yelling at her, Klyucharyov busies himself by inspecting the cave he made. He looks. The cave is deeper, his wife is up to her shoulders in it. She has been digging here for at least half an hour. "It shouldn't be any deeper," he says, still trying not to explode (he's filled with terror that she has come here by herself, it's an animal fear which grabs him in the gut), "widen it out now. So we'll have more space."

"How?" She doesn't understand. "For more space you need to dig to the side." "Which one?" "Whichever you want. It doesn't matter. But not down." He lets her dig a little more, then takes away the shovel. Now he looks around from the inside. There's no need to widen the mouth of the cave any more. A cave should be like a pitcher. A narrow entrance–and only farther in should it widen. At first Klyucharyov uses the pickax like a miner, breaking loose one chunk after another. The earth is a little dry, it breaks apart with a clear dry rustle. Not a word to his wife. He strikes with the pickax until the earth that has crumbled and broken away has piled up to his knees; now Klyucharyov can no longer shift his own center of gravity and with each successive blow he covers more of his body. He almost falls. It's time to stop. He frees his legs. Like a bulldozer, with his hands or, more precisely, with his outstretched palms, he moves the whole mound of earth he had loosened with the pickax to the jaws of the cave; the earth smells of roots and beetles, and from time to time a piece of flint that's turned up scratches his hand. He crawls out.

Trying to step carefully along the slope–oh, the moon's out now–after refastening the flashlight to the same swaying bush branch, he directs its beam to the ground ahead of his feet. Klyucharyov tosses the earth down into the ravine with the shovel, not caring to be quiet, and he distinctly hears the chunks fly into it; they plunge noisily into the bushes (his anger dispersing), break apart, and fly on ahead with a rustle. The whole time his wife has been feeling guilty.

"Don't be mad," she says finally.

He's silent.

"Don't be mad... I'm going. I hope Denis hasn't woken up..."

Silence.

Guiltily, she begins climbing up the slope, falls with a squeak like a bird's, and somehow grabs onto a branch. She scrambles up again. He should be silent a little longer—the sterner Klyucharyov is now, the deeper her sense of guilt about this incident will be and the less likely it is she'll come here again when it's dark without Klyucharyov. It's crazy, after all! But Klyucharyov can't do it. Once you've started to dig a cave, of course, you ought to become at least a little cavemanish and despotic in your relations; otherwise neither you nor your soft-hearted family will escape harm and be able to stick it out. (But it's clear that Klyucharyov is lacking in this regard. He's still only halfway there.) Klyucharyov hurries to his wife and helps her climb out of the ravine. At the top he tells her, "Excuse me. Just a minute," climbs down again, quickly hides the tools and grabs the flashlight. He catches up to her. Gives her the light. He hasn't managed to tell her off, even ineffectually, this man with a pompon on his cap. But it's brighter up here than in the ravine and they both rejoice that you can see so well and so far—as far as their five-story building. It's not night yet! Klyucharyov tells his wife that he went to see the Chursins, Galka sends her greetings, he tells about their deceased neighbor, the old man (do you remember him?) and the bunker he left behind which they're occupying now.

"I'm going to the Pavlovs now," Klyucharyov is thinking out loud. "And I'll come straight home from there."

"But it's getting dark already."

She utters these words with a slight, the very slightest, reproach in her voice, which an outsider would never have sensed, but Klyucharyov hears it, of course, and he's glad, because her reprimand reestablishes their usual relationship with each other—a relationship in which he's guilty and she's right. "Thank God," Klyucharyov thinks. She has gotten over it.

She keeps on talking. Their water hasn't been shut off, but there's no more hot water, we bathed Denis just in time. The millet has run out. The phone? No, it's not working.

* * *

Klyucharyov doesn't walk her home, but watches, of course, as she walks toward their five-story building.

Klyucharyov walks along the river. Keeping his wife in his field of vision, he sits down to take off his shoes and empty out the dirt that's gotten into them (otherwise he won't even make it to the bus). He pulls off his socks and shakes out the sand. He sits there barefoot. All of a sudden he sees that he's sitting by the hole. He almost screams–the gap has closed completely! The earth has pulled together and the bushes right next to the hole are sticking up at almost a thirty-degree angle; they're tilting over, nearly touching the ground, so forcefully had the underground disturbance displaced their roots. The shift didn't disturb the bird-cherry tree, but from the bushes and even the clumps of tall grass you can tell what took place here as clearly as from the needles on measuring devices.

Klyucharyov hadn't planned to go there now, but the thought that he might be cut off forever from the people below drives him toward the hole.

To climb down feet first (as usual) is less dangerous, but he wouldn't get very far now; feet are blind. Klyucharyov is nervous, but he decides to risk it. He crawls in head first. The rush of blood is unpleasant. (And dangerous.) But this way Klyucharyov is able to touch the earth in front of him with his hand and he can twist and squeeze his damp body forward, drawing exhaustively on the experience of crawling things, on the genetic memory of all sorts of flexible spinal columns. With his cheek rubbing against the earth and his hand groping ahead, Klyucharyov crawls down–by touch. There's the neck. It's so tight! He won't get through... The disturbance of the soil bed in this narrow place has already caused not only a flexure but a fracture in the gap, and at most Klyucharyov might just be able to squeeze his head in a bit; he won't be able to crawl like a worm here–the human body is straight. But he does squeeze his head in. Through the noise of blood in his temples and ears he can make out the muffled sounds of the wine cellar, the noise that comes from the tables there, and, after a while, some voices. But it's clear that if he moves down just a little further, in all probability he'll die. He won't be able to get back up. Stop! Don't move. But words are reaching his blocked ears; the words stir him, lift his spirit—they are *sublime words.* Then Klyucharyov distinctly hears singing from a group around a table, *the beloved sounds of a sweet voice,* the strum of a guitar, an argument about spirituality, and someone's deep bass, unexpectedly ebullient, though laced with the harshness of returning sobriety, "Right, right, Vitalik,... another double shot for everyone! Make it fast, guy!" This doesn't upset Klyucharyov in the least; on the contrary, he's overcome by warmth, love, and a passionate human longing to be with them, to be there. Come on, he says, calming himself, meaning: don't listen too much and don't let it hurt you, don't.

The opening has closed, the hole has contracted as much as is possible, and Klyucharyov tries not to think about the enormity of his loss. It's not sitting around the table that he's losing or even the people who sit and think there, it's thought itself—the process of thought. To be sure, none of the people who sit and talk there knows or can know anything with any finality these days, but they all (Klyucharyov included) are trying, and this common attempt is their salvation. Even if it's just an attempt! Oh, no. Don't even think about that. Otherwise you'll perish. For ages people have thought about sublime words. For ages they've given birth to them or at least remembered ones born earlier, and that's why we're able to comprehend them (and in our weakness love them). What else, if not the sting of sublime words, reminds us that he and she (and you and they) are not just creatures who crawl or creep? That he and she (and you also) won't die—what else?... The sublime sky of ceilings over tables where people sit and talk. No, no, Klyucharyov won't start thinking about that. There are sublime words without which he cannot live. (And without which his wife cannot live. And Denis cannot live, for even a person who doesn't understand words can understand that there are words; and this understanding enables him to live. And the Chursins can't go on living. Or that young girl who would have swallowed it near the spot where the traffic light was blinking off and on senselessly. We are our words. Even if we only pass by one another like sickly blue shadows, we are able to pass on words to each another, and in this way we are able to live.)

Trying not to think, driving his thoughts away, Klyucharyov starts to scramble back out when all of a sudden he experiences something he has never in his life experienced before: the sensation of the earth contracting. It catches him around his stomach like a noose, and Klyucharyov realizes that if there's another small shift in the earth he will die. Just like that, he thinks. *So that's it.* But fear prods him on. With his left hand, which he has held next to his body the whole time, precisely in case he'd need to retreat (now he resembles someone swimming sidestroke, swimming in the earth)—with his left hand he grabs convulsively for ledges in the earth. Using all his strength he pulls in his stomach, holds his breath, and at the same time shoves his calloused feet backwards and up through the gap. He writhes and struggles, pushing himself up with pulsating movements. His feet are outside now. His legs are above the ground. A last thrust upward, and his legs fall under their own weight, Klyucharyov's body pulls out by itself, then his head comes out (last of all). Klyucharyov sits there, spitting out dirt. He wipes his eyes which are full of sand. And breathes and breathes.

This has all taken a very short time, it seems. In any case, after wiping the dirt from his eyes, Klyucharyov sees that his wife is still walking up the bluish-gray asphalt path. She has reached the building now. Maybe it's dark between the buildings and that's why his wife has turned on the flashlight—Klyucharyov sees the slanting elliptical patch of light beside her feet on the dark road.

His wife is near the second five-story building now. (He might have been able to get there, might have crawled and pushed through, scraping his cheek and bloodying his ear, but the earth could have shifted after he crawled through and not before, and Klyucharyov would have been left there, cut off, separated from this darkening street where his wife now walks and where Denis is, such an enormous and good boy, and the dead Pavlov, and where it's impossible to buy either a battery or a nail on the dark streets.)

Klyucharyov bends down and shouts into the hole, which has closed completely, "Hey!... Hey-ey!... Hey-ey!" This is his fury, it's pointless now, but even his furious shout does not get through. He hears nothing in reply. (And the only information he has sent is a few pebbles and some sand which fell down while Klyucharyov was trying to push his way through. The waiter swept it up without even complaining.) Klyucharyov's wife is next to their building now. The spot of light from her flashlight has been extinguished; since she's near home she's probably saving the battery's last breath. But the battery could have run down by itself, gone dead. As far as Klyucharyov was able to see, his wife hadn't looked back while walking–she'd been lost in thought. She won't go out on the street by herself any more. She won't leave the apartment. (If he wakes up and no one is right there, Denis cries out; he has a simple nature, he'll open a window looking out on the street and call in a crying voice, "Mama! Mama!..." a gift to anyone who loves profit and easy pickings. An empty, desolate street. A child's cry–what could be easier!)

3

ENGINEER PAVLOV's DOOR. There it is. Pavlov told Klyucharyov about the door when he was still alive. In one of his quiet moments, at the height of his fear, Pavlov invented this door–so simple and so brilliant (but is it simpler and more brilliant than the cave?). Klyucharyov notices the delicate design of metallic strips and on them, like periods, the tiny openings that run through the door–distinctive pores, out of which small doses of death can be sprayed from behind the door. Small but effective. (The people in the mob should believe this. The tiny holes are for them.) The door is able to exhale through its metal pores, because behind the door is a rather small, but again effective, X-ray "cannon." A sign on the door in large letters explains, as if to say, There's nothing secret here, guys, don't have any illusions. BEHIND THIS DOOR THERE'S A "CANNON"; TWO SECONDS IN FRONT OF THE DOOR EQUALS 2000 ROENTGEN RAYS; FOUR SECONDS–4000 ROENTGEN RAYS. Engineer Pavlov left no other words, figuring that even without further explanation the sign would be quite clear to those who might take it into their head to break down the door (however professional and fast and emboldened by alcohol they might be).

Klyucharyov rings the door bell and seconds pass. Olya Pavlov, who has already had time to come to the door and look through the peephole, must be thinking, should I kill Klyucharyov with the switch or, since I recognize him, simply open the door?... She opens the door, still in tears, her nose red from weeping. "Come in. You took so long!..." And, indeed, Chursin's already here. Chursin is sitting at the table with a map of the city spread out in front of him, marking with a dark pencil the routes of the buses that are still running.

Olya immediately begins to hurry them, "Let's not waste time, let's get moving, look how fast it's getting dark!" But at the same time she serves everyone a cup of tea. She's wearing an apron. Her stomach is a mound–she's in her sixth, or is it her seventh or even eighth month?

There's an argument after tea. Chursin, who had come here his own way, insists that Bus 42's route has been shortened and it won't meet No. 291. He suggests walking two blocks over to the movie theater and boarding No. 295 directly–that would take them almost straight to the medical institute. Klyucharyov's against this: the theater has been vacant a long time, and so the bus, especially one with such a long route as 295, might have a shorter route now that skips the movie theater. "What will we do then?"

"But it does go there," Chursin insists.

"You'll see."

Chursin is certain. He's wearing his old peaked cap, which he has pulled down over his forehead. He puts this cap on when he's ready for a no-holds-barred battle. (In a battle for survival the cap calls forth his reserves of inner strength, reawakening his life in the orphanage. There's a real change in his whole appearance and manner, even in his speech.)

Olya Pavlova changes her clothes and they get ready to leave. She goes and gets a bag and puts white sheets in it. "They might prove useful," she says quietly (clearly repeating a wise phrase she has heard about something else) and begins to sob loudly. That is, the sheets are needed to wrap him, what else? In order to distract her thoughts from the white sheets Klyucharyov poses a question: "Olya, what's happened to the machine? Where's the 'cannon?'" (Obviously, he knows that no such "cannon" exists. But maybe there's at least some contraption that flashes brightly. So that something streams out from the door through the holes.)

"Pavlov didn't manage to finish it."

"But I don't even see a beginning."

They stand at the door for a minute before leaving (there's not the slightest trace of any contraption). The idea that Pavlov hadn't really done anything strikes Klyucharyov like a bolt of lightning. The mind of a prankster. Cheerful and sly. Sometimes he would fall into high drama and say that no hole would tempt him for long, and no matter what happened he'd stay out on the streets when it started to get dark. And he did.

BUS NO. 295 is approaching and the passenger car is shimmering with light. It's not yet night, but the bus is already driving with its lights on, of course. There are a dozen policemen on the bus, they're being assigned to different posts. At every third stop a certain number of policemen get off. Usually two. A pair. They stopped using single guards everywhere a long time ago—too easy a target.

Olya Pavlova is telling about her husband. They didn't call her, the call went to the telephone station, where the power supply was already being cut. The station was being temporarily shut down. From one minute to the next units were disconnected, and they called Olya Pavlova from the monitoring phone and shouted into the receiver that her Pavlov had collapsed right on the street. A heart attack. People from the medical institute had picked him up, they had a morgue—all this was shouted to her in great haste so that half the words were swallowed up, and yet she had to thank them for this, be very thankful... Olya is crying, "And why would people from the medical institute pick up the homeless from the streets? Just to dissect them..."

"Oh, come on!" Klyucharyov and Chursin cut her short.

They are comforting her, "Try not to cry..."

The motor drones from overexertion; the bus is climbing a hill, which means they're already out of the first district.

At the bus stop a brawny, cold-blooded type boards. He's wearing a new quilted jacket and short boots (And it looks as if he has a knife in one. He's the sort even the police fear—who's out every night hunting for police guns). A strong man, about thirty-five, with bright gray eyes that search at leisure for a victim. He sits and looks tough while suppressing a grin. At one of the stops he gets off and steps down into the semidarkness as if he's going home. The hour is his.

No one announces the stops; the driver keeps quiet.

Klyucharyov continually looks out the window in order to orient himself and decipher the names of the stops on the signs. In the semidarkness he has glimpses of abandoned playgrounds where no children have played for a long time. Yet the empty swings are a comforting presence. Store windows stretch on and on, one after another, flashing signs with enormous letters: OUT OF STOCK. PLEASE DO NOT BREAK THE GLASS, but the windows are broken, of course. The holes made by the stones shine and long cracks branch out from them. Half of a brick is stuck in the glass (it had broken the first pane and stuck in the second); its flying power exhausted, it has lodged there and protrudes from the glass, and two-meter-long cracks fan out from it like rays from the sun.

Only the three of them are left on the bus.

At one of the stops the bus brakes suddenly and their heads jerk forward. Olya Pavlova immediately puts her hands over her stomach for protection.

The bus has stopped. The doors are open. It's the end of the road—this is made clear without any words, even though the bus route doesn't end at this stop, and for this reason, as they're leaving, all three go to the driver's cab to try their luck. "We have to go further," Klyucharyov pressures him, but the driver just shakes his head. "No, I'm not going." No, he won't go any further. Chursin won't stop, "But she's pregnant! Can't you see?..."

"Sure she's pregnant!" the driver yells, his anger suddenly flashing out at these intellectuals who were and are responsible for everything. "Sure I can see she's pregnant! If she didn't have that belly, you'd have all crawled off into your holes a long time ago! Hidden away there!"

This class anger is crude, as usual, but, then, when targeting something it only aims at a crude, approximate precision. He'd probably been listening to their conversation and inasmuch as they hadn't been swearing or talking about primuses and grub, it was clear that they were the ones who had brought the country to ruin. Destroyed it! (If not sold it out.)

But you can understand the driver as well (Klyucharyov realizes this at once, he's quick to excuse him), because directly on the other side of the small square that the bus driver has hesitated to cross is an area of dark, deserted streets known to be dangerous, where there are just a few buildings and the unfinished medical institute complex.

"So go, then, you bastard!..." yells Chursin, who just five minutes earlier had placed so much hope in his cap. (He'd expected it to make him look more common, perhaps turn him into some kind of workingman.)

They stand there.

The bus makes a slow U-turn. As the driver's cab is circling around, it turns up opposite them for a moment or two. The driver puts on the brake, and shouts that he'd already driven through those deserted streets and he's had enough! "I drove there yesterday!" In the darkness he was immediately surrounded by toughs and they had stolen his gas. Right from the gas tank. And, what's more, they took away the supper his wife had given him to take to work. They took his last two cigarettes. They snatched his belt. And some son of a bitch ordered him to take off his shoes, but when he saw that the shoes weren't in very good condition, he'd just pissed in them. "A real wise guy, the fucker!..."

The driver screams all this over the roar his bus makes as it turns, over the backfire from the exhaust pipe.

"Go on, get out of here, scum! Too bad they didn't piss on your head!" Chursin yells straight in his face. He doesn't excuse himself or back down. Once it comes to the surface, class anger makes everything on both sides simpler and more nasty.

They continue to shout at each other over the roar of the motor, until the bus finally takes off on its return route.

The crossing is deserted.

For a rather long time they walk in silence. Olya Pavlova holds onto Chursin's arm—it's so quiet and desolate here. Klyucharyov is carrying her bag.

In this most absolute quiet, from somewhere far away—though precisely that part of the city they are heading for—a sound lifts in the air and drifts unevenly toward them. This sound can't be compared with anything (it's convenient to compare it with the sound of oncoming waves, but there's little similarity—the image is strained). This sound is unique. A drumming and a hum flow together into one grating whir. From far away it's immediately recognizable to every human ear: the mob.

With each second the shuffle of thousands of feet comes closer; yet it still all seems to be taking place somewhere far away, and so it is all the more surprising when this shuffle of feet and droning suddenly materialize into a large group of people. "Oh, my God!" shouts Olya Pavlova. A stream of people has appeared in an instant. People moving in a hurry, and in their rush they are pressing tightly together, shoulder to shoulder. The stream is still not large, but what's coming after them?

Klyucharyov, Chursin, and Olya come to a stop. They look—a stream of people is emerging from behind a building, skirting the building so closely that their shoulders have probably already worn the corner and walls down to the bricks. Why, in accordance with the law of motion brought to a standstill, must the mob turn here and not there? No one knows. Some people break loose and leap out of the crush, separating themselves from the general whirl, and then—with relative freedom—they immediately press onward, almost at a run (A rush forward, rousing shouts! The trampling of feet on the pavement!). Over the heads of those running in front you can see another stream of people now. Behind them comes a third stream.

"We can cut in between, but then we'll immediately run into the big mob. They'll trample everything in their path! We won't be able to get out," Klyucharyov says.

Chursin tosses his cigarette butt away and spits.

"But otherwise we won't get through at all."

"What if we go through the courtyards?"

There's no time to argue—they have to decide on something. They both look at Olya Pavlova, as if she can decide or at least give them some signal. But Olya doesn't say a word, of course; her eyes stare ahead blankly, in panic.

They take a roundabout way. The buildings are deserted and silent. The yards as well: the children's swings are vacant, the clotheslines empty. The benches the old women sit on near the entranceway are also vacant. Two dogs spring out from somewhere and rush past, "Shoo! Shoo!" Chursin shouts, and Olya Pavlova clings to Klyucharyov in fear. Chursin cups his hands around his mouth and yells to the windows of the buildings, "Hey-ey!" The next minute drags on forever. Then in one dark window the flat shadow of a face appears. The advice comes through a small windowpane, "You won't get through here. Take the next left. And keep on going till you reach the wall!"

The buildings with their dead glass eyes stretch on without end and the endless courtyards are empty, but as soon as Chursin, Klyucharyov, and Olya come out in a passageway between the buildings, they hear that same shuffle of thousands of feet on the pavement and the muffled drone (not yet a roar) of the mob. The temporary absence of trampling was deceptive. In order to determine the direction of the approaching drone, they skirt around the courtyards again, but now they come face to face with a row of attached garages. This way is dangerous, it might end abruptly and where could they go then?... Courtyards... Children's playlots. A sandbox and discarded toy shovels. And the row of garages still goes on (a garage door that's been broken in, no car, of course). Suddenly they notice a drunk. He's short and thin, and he starts following them, whining, "Co-Co-com-mrades. D-don't... don't... leave me..."

Klyucharyov and Chursin don't respond.

The drunk trails behind them, muttering something about losing a lottery ticket and how a bus has just knocked him down, apparently even run him over, so that now his "insides are all coming out."

"Don't whine," Chursin brushes him off sternly.

They've reached a high stone wall. On the other side must be the square they need to cross before the crowd gets there. At the wall the lush begins to whine with particular insistence, he clings, gets in their way, hangs onto them, fearing that they will leave him here forever. There's no time. His whining annoys them to the point that Chursin and Klyucharyov sit him down, toss him up on the wall like a sack, and help him roll over to the other side.

But Olya is the main thing. Klyucharyov has found a board and leans it against the wall. The board's a little too short and the slope is quite steep. Olya leans on Chursin's hands for support and makes her way up the board while Chursin stands on the ground. Chursin's arms aren't long enough, they get tired. The board feels heavier with each of her steps, but Klyucharyov is sitting astride the stone wall now, holding his hands out to her from above—come on... just a bit more. He stretches out and catches Olya and helps her sit on the edge of the wall. Klyucharyov is wet, he's soaking with sweat as he holds Olya with both hands and helps her lower herself down slowly. "Just don't drop. Don't fall. Be patient. I'll let you down almost to the ground," Klyucharyov repeats. Just a little more—and his stomach will burst from the strain. But Chursin is already over the wall, he has jumped down, and he takes all the living weight of Olya and her stomach into his arms.

"Faster!" Klyucharyov urges.

From the top of the wall, before he jumps down Klyucharyov can see farther than they can. A square lies ahead and an enormous crowd pours into it, but the upper end of the square is still empty, it's free of people, they must hurry.

The trample of thousands and thousands of feet fills their ears and plugs them. Together the three rush toward the unoccupied space—it's crucial to reach the middle of the square at least (so that when they're pushed out, it will be to the other side). The mob is running at them. They don't collide because the front runners are scattered: there are still patches of space between people, and insofar as Klyucharyov, Chursin, and Olya try to avoid them, the runners try not to hit them or knock them down. Because of these patches, these vacuums in the mob, the three are able to keep moving even when the unavoidable collisions of body against body begin. "I can't go on!" says Olya Pavlova. She stumbles and suddenly sits down, clasping her belly with her arms and breathing heavily. "You're crazy!" Chursin shouts and grabs her hand.

She sobs, "I ca-an't!"

Klyucharyov and Chursin bend down and try to pull her up by the arms, they plead and urge her at least to get up. People are running around them and running into them, knocking them off balance. The mob is getting denser; they are being crushed and dragged and—somehow Olya

Pavlova does get up—constantly jabbed by elbows, nudged and shoved. The hot breath of the mob is in their faces. The light is eclipsed. They're surrounded by heads and shoulders and jackets. Klyucharyov protects Olya; they stand next to each other, holding on to each other tightly. They are joined together, they've become a single body, but this does not help them push forward.

"Chursin! Chursin!" Klyucharyov calls.

But he has already been carried away from them. They can't see him. There's a roar and a drone on all sides. The dense mob is becoming denser, it's pressing in on them. "Don't let yourself be pulled away. Hold on to me. Hold on to me," Klyucharyov urges Olya, and he all but shoves her into a small space that has formed in front of them (thinking, are they at the middle yet?). Olya is breathing into his face, into his neck. She acts brave. It feels as if they've reached the other side now and Klyucharyov decides not to push through the crowd any more but to submit to it to some degree. Right away everything becomes easier. The mob presses and squeezes and carries them in some definite pattern forward and to the side, it carries them along a kind of almost tangible smooth curve. Holding on to each other, they take a step or two into a patch of space, then submit to the flow again; they're caught up in the mob like wood chips and carried off the way a river would take them. Over heads and caps Klyucharyov can already see the other side of the square: little by little the buildings on the other side draw near—it's as if a slow current is tossing Klyucharyov and Olya up onto the bank of a river.

The faces of the mob are hard and dark. The mob isn't a monolith—it's made up of diverse beings, but all the same it remains a mob, with all its unpredictability and heightened suggestibility. Faces suddenly turn white from anger and spite, clenched fists await, and the blows are savage, right between the eyes. People are wedged in, and they wedge in others. Every minute there are skirmishes, but all these skirmishes recede into the background before the essential trait of the mob: its common uniformity, which is why the mob doesn't answer to anyone but itself when it tramples anyone who's not part of it. Fortunately, the movement of Klyucharyov and Olya goes unnoticed: it's dissolved in the movement of the mob, intrinsically concealed. They are carried along by the mob. They're a part of it. Olya is shivering. Her teeth are chattering feverishly from the terror she's living through. "For the rest of my life. The rest of my life..." Olya Pavlova repeats, meaning she'll always remember this, she'll never forget.

At a certain moment, sticking out his neck, Klyucharyov sees Chursin, who can't break out of a bottleneck that has formed around a lamppost. Chursin is making a desperate effort to get out, but as soon as he elbows his way out to the side he is immediately dragged back along with the entire mass. He's dragged with such force that he has to make another grab for the lamppost. "Chur-siiin!" Klyucharyov yells, but Chursin doesn't hear him. For one more moment Klyucharyov sees his face, damp from the struggling and the muscular strain, sees his cap, but then Klyucharyov and Olya are carried farther away, Chursin is torn from the lamp, and his face with the cap pulled over the forehead disappears, borne away by the mob.

They've already gotten their bearings, Olya Pavlova and Klyucharyov. The thick of the crowd is behind them, sometimes they're pushed, but it's like the beat of a weak pulse. One might say that they are now striding along side by side.

They are standing on the other side, near one of the buildings. Waiting. Beneath his pants Klyucharyov's legs feel wet, as if the lower half of his body has been in a sauna—it feels warmer than his head and chest. He has oriented himself now and points out the medical institute complex to Olya, "Over there..." but the mob is still moving past. The mob is pushing on. Klyucharyov and Olya huddle in a small sidestreet, which provides them refuge, while the swelling mob presses forward. "Aa-aaa. Uu-uuuu..." the many-voiced, many-footed presence surges all about, and nothing can contain it except the rigid stone bodies of the buildings on the left and right. Thank God, Chursin appears. Without his cap and with the stunned face of a man who has just been saved by a miracle rather than his past in the orphanage. And the mob surges ahead, wave after wave.

The three of them are walking together again—along a small street, intent on their sad duty. Their pace quickens (after the roar of the crowd) as they plunge ever deeper into that very quiet they had feared.

The streets are empty again. The sky darkens. It's dusk.

They find the building they need (someone from here had called the telephone station, and from there they had relayed the message to Olya). They're only allowed to go as far as a certain partition, a man sits behind it with a gun, like a watchman. They take a long time explaining across the partition who they are and why they've come. "Semyonych!..." the man shouts to some Semyonych, shouting shrilly into the empty building, and a short little man in a quilted jacket appears, carrying enormous rusty keys on a steel ring. "Hello there," Semyonych says quite simply (and quite warmly); he gives a sign with his hand for them to come, and without any further impediment they follow him to the morgue. A modest little building some distance away.

From the very beginning of their excursion, it's been clear to Klyucharyov that they obviously won't be able to take Pavlov's body anywhere this evening (how? and where to?) and that they'll have to bury him right here. And for that reason, as he searches for an opportunity and contact, Klyucharyov talks with Semyonych about this and that; he speaks good-naturedly and from the heart, and Semyonych also speaks good-naturedly, blurting out, "Huh-uh" from time to time in place of an answer. They are walking side by side. Olya Pavlova walks behind them, overcome by tears—you can hear the cycle of her sobs, a short stifled cry followed by uncontrollable weeping. But Chursin is with her, he puts his arm around her shoulder and comforts her.

Jingling his bunch of keys, the copper-faced Semyonych gives Olya a piece of paper to sign. But they won't let her inside, of course. Chursin goes in, then Klyucharyov. Semyonych turns on the light and points—they quickly take their prankish Pavlov, who is lying on the front table, and wrap him in one of the sheets. Pavlov is lying in ice, completely frozen; he's wearing pants, a shirt and a jacket, and his tie, as always, is flung back irreverently to one side. After wrapping him in the first sheet, they place him on the second one and, gripping the corners tightly, they carry him out–Chursin in front, Klyucharyov behind. Olya stands and buries her face in her hands.

The rest goes quickly. Semyonych asks again if they have a car (whoever has a car parks it quietly at dark, and it sits somewhere with the other cars, as if abandoned and out of gas too). But, indeed, there's no car. Then Semyonych tells them that in back of the second institute building there's a small church that's been destroyed. There's a row of old graves there. The day before yesterday he, Semyonych, had buried a young fellow there who had been trampled by the mob.

The old church might be torn down some day, of course; they might replace it with a new building and Olya would be left without a grave for her husband. But there isn't a better choice. Consequently, Klyucharyov keeps quiet (not a word to Olya), and Chursin keeps quiet too. Semyonych offers to go with them. He gets hold of an old hospital stretcher from somewhere in order to make the move easier. Alternating first with Chursin, then with Klyucharyov, he helps them carry in turn. He's remarkable, this Semyonych, one of the last professionals doing a job honestly. Klyucharyov carries the back end and Semyonych goes in front, a man of small stature in an old quilted jacket, with a head of gray hair.

The church is in ruins, even more desecrated by the rubbish left behind. It had been a storehouse, then they'd decided not to use it even for storage. As soon as they see people, the ravens fly up in concert; one of them soars and then swings back and forth on a tall bar that stands in place of a cross. Semyonych takes a shovel from the bushes and says he'll do the digging, he's better at it. But they dig too, taking his place. The pit becomes deep quickly; at first its opening is like a gap, like an ordinary hole, then for a time

the pit is spacious and suggests the possibility of a cave, but in the end the deadly form of four right-angled corners conquers the space of the earth and the pit becomes what it now will be—a grave. The cave of their Pavlov, it is given to him, the earth for his bed. Olya has fallen over the cold body; she has freed his head and is kissing it. Everything is over. They lower him without a coffin, wrapped in the sheet. They strew dirt upon his grave. And when their quickly made mound is finished, they stand there, parted from him.

Semyonych sees them back, swinging the keys and repeating to Olya that he will plant a "splendid wild rose" here "as a remembrance"; he'll find a large, healthy bush and transplant it on top of the grave. Semyonych becomes too talkative in parting, and all the while he releases a flow of goodwill, which, he thinks, he hasn't managed to give them enough of during their brief shared labor.

After they see Olya home, they stand for a while at the entrance to her building—Olya herself, Chursin and Klyucharyov. The men tell each other they have to stick together. Chursin assures them that his elderly neighbor's bunker will house them all perfectly well and that if things become dangerous they should all come to him immediately, and, for his part, Klyucharyov reports that he's digging out a cave, it's in an excellent location, well-hidden, there's a brook nearby, the water's clear... They keep on inviting each other like this, but gradually the familiar sensation of separation makes itself felt. Because it's more dangerous to be together. And although they sincerely say yes, yes, yes, let's stick together, let's stay together, let's figure things out together, with each passing moment they sense all the more that their kind words are just their hope and in another moment they'll part. They stop talking. For reasons independent of the inclinations of their souls, Chursin is putting his hopes on the bunker, Klyucharyov on the cave, and Olya Pavlova on her frightening door with its warning about the "cannon." There's a feeling of sadness. It seems paradoxical, yet nature is telling them not to stay together now in order to survive, but, on the contrary, to stay separated, to hide themselves in their nooks, to make themselves smaller and less conspicuous, for it is precisely those who have scattered, those who have become like specks of dust, who have the greatest chance to survive and emerge unscathed.

Olya Pavlova stands there lost in thought. (She's still at the grave.)

They ask her, "How will you have the baby? Is your sister coming?..."

She nods. Yes, her sister has promised, her older sister will come when it's time and she'll help. That's important. Naturally, Klyucharyov's wife and Chursin's wife will help, too. But how will they get in touch? How will they know, if there's no telephone and no mail?... If they could just exchange a word or two from time to time, where bus No. 28 circles around, let's say. This circle (more or less) is close to us all. Yes, yes, if something goes wrong or something very important happens, then we'll meet at No. 28...

THE DARK COMES QUICKLY, but it's not night yet. Maybe the darkness seems greater than it really is because as Klyucharyov walks along a completely deserted street two windows among the thousand dark windows all of a sudden light up and virtually shoot into his eyes (someone accidentally turned on the lights in an apartment, then suddenly remembered and turned them off immediately). Klyucharyov is involuntarily dazzled by the flash, and, as often happens in semidarkness, he's left blinded for a while. It's like walking at night.

His eyes still can't see and Klyucharyov bumps into someone. Klyucharyov immediately jumps aside, but the man runs off too. He hadn't seen Klyucharyov either, because he'd been squatting down, rummaging through the pockets of someone lying on the pavement, probably dead drunk. The man runs off. But seeing that Klyucharyov has passed on, he quickly returns to his victim.

"Get outta here!" Bolder now, he yells out in a hoarse voice after Klyucharyov.

He sits down on the slumped-over man and empties the jacket pockets one by one. He finishes with the jacket and goes through the pants. He throws some of his pickings off to the side and happily pockets something else for himself. The drunk gives no sign of life. Maybe he's dead.

Klyucharyov goes on alone, he doesn't meet anyone else. It's dusk. There's only the deserted street and the muted sound of his own steps.

4

THE GAP HAS WIDENED A LITTLE. It's evident. Every time he's ready to go down, as he sits on the edge with his legs lowered into the hole, Klyucharyov dumps everything out of his pockets beforehand so that he won't wound himself while pushing through—his pen, his apartment keys, a change purse. Klyucharyov wraps these things up in a small bag, which he ties like a package and attaches to his foot at the ankle so that the package hangs from his foot and unobtrusively goes deeper and deeper into the hole by itself, ahead of him. But the sharp stones can't be hidden in a package—there's no protection against them. When his body jerks (and this is inevitable) Klyucharyov stops pushing and begins to coil downwards, first with his knees and buttocks, then with his shoulders, making circular motions, breathing loudly all the while, and now and then crying out when something suddenly hurts. A piece of flint or a small stone (sometimes the size of a nut) breaks loose from the soil bed and settles between Klyucharyov's ribs and the narrow neck, causing unbearable pain. The important thing at such times is to not to jerk and to remember to breathe, otherwise you'll instinctively start to scramble back up again in panic like someone drowning, and all your work will have been for nothing–you'll get your breath back and have to go down again. Klyucharyov twists his left hand in and tries to grab the flint. There's not a minute to lose–once it has ripped open the skin, a small stone can easily get into the wound and that really kills. He's anxious. At the same time, Klyucharyov exhales all the air he can from his lungs, so that the stone that's just been unwedged for a moment will slip further down under its own gravity. Either the stone will fall down by itself (as it does now), or Klyucharyov's bent left hand will manage to find the loosened stone and grab it with his fingers. That's how important the breathing is. While he exhales the air from his lungs again, Klyucharyov pulls in as much as he can–and the stone flies down. Moreover, with his lungs empty once more, with a jerk Klyucharyov follows the stone, coiling his way down a distance of almost half a meter. There's a pain in his side–the stone has torn through the bandage, injuring his skin, but be that as it may, Klyucharyov has already passed through the narrow part of the gap.

He tries to expand now, he braces himself against the sides with his elbows, since the gap is wide now and his feet don't touch the earth–they hang. Another push and Klyucharyov has squeezed through completely, he hovers in the air. He is hanging over open space and groping about with his feet for the top rung of the stairway. Neither his left nor his right foot can find anything (Klyucharyov would need to lower his head, just a little, in order to see). Fortunately, a piece of armature in the ceiling juts out right from the hole and Klyucharyov, who has started to slip, grasps on to it with his hands. He can hang more securely now. And he can see. People are eating and drinking below–there's the usual noise and commotion. The ladder-stairway with its supporting frame has been moved off to one side in order to make room for several small tables for the guests.

"Hey!" Klyucharyov calls down. (But not too loudly; he finds it awkward and not very civilized to interrupt people who are absorbed in their food and conversation). That's it, then. They've set up tables, they're drinking and arguing and they've simply moved the stairway off to the side, they've forgotten. There are two new small tables. They're almost straight below the dangling Klyucharyov.

"Hey! Hey-ey!"

He might crush them. For a second Klyucharyov lets go with one hand and scrapes away some pebbles and earth with his fingers and throws them down, aiming away from the table, of course, and at the man sitting at the far end. He misses. Once more. This time Klyucharyov chooses only pebbles, he lets the earth fall out from in between his fingers and flings only a handful of pebbles at a large solid man who's just raised his glass of vodka. Bull's-eye. Puzzled, the guy looks to the left and right and then up at last.

"Oho!" he cries out. "Look!..."

Whereupon the lady with him and then the others at the table holler and point out Klyucharyov to each other while he's sticking to the ceiling. The man has put down his vodka, set down his fork with a piece of fish, and gotten up. A waiter runs over to help and together they begin rolling the ladder with its supporting frame. The frame won't budge, it's too heavy, so two more bearded intellectuals rush over to help. Slightly drunk and expansively good-natured, they laugh at the dangling Klyucharyov and shove the waiter aside with a "get back to your own work, twerp"—and all together they give the frame a vigorous push, rolling it under Klyucharyov with so much momentum that the top step of the ladder almost hits his legs. His feet find a support. As Klyucharyov climbs down, at each rung he feels a slight quivering in his legs. After the strain of hanging for so long, his diaphragm won't relax, he twitches and then he gets the hiccups as well. But he's already surrounded, they slap him on the shoulders and take him around to one table, to another and even a third, "Here! Over here! To us!" They give Klyucharyov mineral water and Pepsi to get rid of his rather indelicate hiccups, but someone yells that it's not the right thing, you need cognac,

cognac's best! Klyucharyov still can't recognize anyone's face.

"You must be hungry! Have something to eat!... There's an excellent fillet today, have some!" people are speaking from all sides. Someone hands him a plate and a glass of vodka, and Klyucharyov drinks and chews and gradually recovers.

They resume their conversation (about Dostoevsky, about not wanting a fortune that is built on the misfortune of others, even a small one—a familiar opener), and within a few minutes Klyucharyov's soul is focused on their sublime words. They sit and talk. Spiritual energies tend to merge when people sit at a table and talk, and Klyucharyov, who felt numb (dead) on those desolate streets where the only active energy was the thief who sat on a victim and rummaged in his pockets—the numb Klyucharyov feels the presence of words. Like a fish landing in water again, he revives. This is what he had come for.

The lighting is marvelous. Klyucharyov is happy to see faces. On the half-dark streets he has learned to be satisfied with a faint patch of face and a smudged line of cheekbone, and so he now almost involuntarily takes in the richness of each human face, male and female alike.

The flow of sublime words has subsided. Our interactions cannot be continuously sublime, just as one can't look at the stars all night. The soul stretches, gives a shudder, takes a deep breath—and that's enough. The mechanics of every conversation are such that after a brief flash of spirit comes small talk, chatter about everyday concerns, and ironic comments on them; information is exchanged and mulled over and over at length, and only from afar does the spirit flash again, perhaps strongly or perhaps briefly, like a momentary explosion, but the human interaction which makes us receptive to it sometimes lingers for the sake of even this momentary flash.

A belief that we are *together* (both there on the dark streets and here at the table), and a belief that this together has been part of our essence from the very beginning... What is this? What's this about?... The man speaking is Georgy N., he's young and squirming with impatience. Klyucharyov doesn't know him well. Georgy N. steers everyone's attention to Klyucharyov by asking, "Is there still electricity?... Don't you have to move around in total darkness up there?"

What can you tell him? How can you describe the light from a single streetlamp one hundred meters away on the distant underground crossing of an empty street?... As he answers, Klyucharyov mechanically pulls at his shirt. It's stuck to the clotted blood and he tears it off; piece by piece, in centimeters, Klyucharyov rips the shirt away from his body (it doesn't hurt, and it's smart to do it, so that the shirt won't dry onto the wounds). Georgy N. suddenly breaks out in a fit of coughing (pain of another kind) and when the coughing dies down and Georgy takes the handkerchief from his mouth Klyucharyov notices a clot of blood on the handkerchief. The blood's not from his body but from his throat. It's rather light despite being low in oxygen. Georgy N. hastily throws the handkerchief into his large and respectable briefcase, hides it there, and pulls out another. And as if nothing happened, he sits and strokes his young whiskers with the handkerchief.

"We need more drinks. Sergei, tell the waiter double shots for everyone."

"And a few appetizers?"

"Appetizers, too."

And he tunes into their conversation again, "Allow me to disagree, Sergei..."

A man with a red scarf whom Klyucharyov doesn't know starts off on a new flawless run of words—without passion, however. For the time being the spirit has abandoned the speakers; yet they still maintain their standards of language. (In order for the spirit to have some place to return to—like coals that a breeze might fan.)

"...And if misery does exist, then it's a common misery. Let's just for once examine the negative, adverse connotation of the word 'common.' What are we afraid of? What we're afraid of now is that we are common and we're bound by that commonality—if there's hunger, unrest on the streets, pogroms and murders out in the open, then the mob will completely lose its mind. *That* will grab hold of us all, that's what commonality is. We don't believe in the police or the army or even in tanks on the street, because the police, the army, and the tanks are exactly like us. They're certain to be late. They're one hundred percent certain to be too late, because they and the crowd are one..."

An elderly man objects (somewhat grumpily) to what's been said. He says that gloom is also a trait common to us today and we shouldn't give in to it.

Suddenly a woman (who was quiet until now) makes a switch to history, "Is the commonality of the present not related to the Russian peasant commune—I mean the collective thinking in the village commune."

One could plunge the conversation even further into the depths of the ages, to backwaters and groves that have fallen silent, to more healthy general conclusions. A departure into antiquity keeps the coals burning. From time to time when thought takes wing from the bed of history, it is restructured by the quantum of old energy it has seized there. For spirit is enriched above all by the chaos of different opinions.

Klyucharyov stands up. He has recovered his breath, had a nip of fresh air; now he can go on living. He can think about his concrete petty cares: get tea, buy batteries, buy kerosene, what else?... Since he's getting ready to leave, they want to drink to his health. (And since he's already up, they'll get up too and make a standing toast.)

Not giving the topic a rest, the young Georgy N. hurriedly says, "We are bound by existence in a swarm, like bees. And if we perish, we'll all perish suddenly like bees. No matter where we may be at the time (above or below—it doesn't matter!). Give me just another minute. I'm so happy that we're standing to drink together here. As if we're in flight. Do you know how a swarm of bees perishes? The bees take off all together and shoot straight up, they make a last run through the air, fly their last flight, then plunge all together onto the ground and the grass, their little legs up and–don't look!–the last shudder is not a pretty picture..."

SHOPPING. The abundance of light is overwhelming. Sometimes the lamps lose the symmetry of the street and collapse into clusters before his eyes–a fiery waterfall, the play of fire–just a little more, and Klyucharyov will feel the smell of pine needles in the air, Christmas trees with shaggy boughs, and childhood.

The stores are brightly decorated at sale time. (After all, how to attract is also a game from childhood.) The stores are stuffed with things. Whatever you want. And how you want it. They're bursting with goods. True, the salesclerks are arrogant and a little too smug. Whenever there are few customers (and there are almost no customers), the salesman should be, if not polite, then obliging, say, in a European manner–but, then again, this isn't Europe or even emigration. The salesman helps Klyucharyov choose a small kerosene stove, but as soon as Klyucharyov pays, he tosses him a box with the bright label of the firm on it so that he can pack it up (Wrap it yourself! You won't break your hands!). The box doesn't reach Klyucharyov. The salesman has turned away and buried his head in a newspaper.

Klyucharyov needs ordinary coarse gray cloth to cover the cave he's digging on the slope to the river. The salesman in the neighboring shop is much more polite–he calls out and invites him in. His small store is even more glittery inside than outside. There are neon arrows everywhere, in various colors, advertising the particular material they're propped against. It's wonderful material, attractive and bright, but Klyucharyov needs something completely different. "We can roll the material up for you. It's easy to carry, like a fishing rod. A rod with its line wound!" the salesman jokes, giving him an attentive, knowing look. Maybe beneath Klyucharyov's sweater he sees the outline of the bandage stretching across his scraped body (and, after all, "easy to carry" explicitly means "get it through the gap, push it through the hole, the ease of narrowness"). Klyucharyov (he's not making any secret about his purchases) explains that he needs gray; if not dark, then at least a subdued color that won't attract attention from a distance, even if some curious head should stick itself into the cave. If your material's colored, then let it be the shade of rain and shriveled black leaves and wet snow.

"No," the salesman shakes his head.

And though he understands Klyucharyov, he's unable to help him, and he repeats, "No."

And then yells to Klyucharyov, as he's on his way out, "You won't find it anywhere, why would we carry such worthless stuff?! It gets dirty so easily! The first time it rains you'll trample on the material and ruin it without even noticing!"

Someone touches Klyucharyov on the shoulder. Excuse me. Just a minute... It's the salesman from the shop, not the one with the intelligent look, but the first one, the rude one, from whom Klyucharyov bought the batteries and the small kerosene stove. Probably for the last ten minutes Klyucharyov's kerosene stove ("The smallest one. And preferably one that's narrow...") had been lazily floating around in his mind and now it reached consciousness.

"Listen," the salesman lowers his voice to a whisper. "Listen. Are you heading back up?"

Klyucharyov nods.

"I have a favor to ask. Don't refuse... Call this number," he gives Klyucharyov (as a gift) another flashlight battery that has a seven-figure phone number clearly written on it. "Tell them Valentin Andreyevich sends greetings. Valentin Andreyevich—that's me. Just greetings. I won't ask for anything else. Just these four words—to say I'm alive and well..."

The smug and rude look on his face has disappeared completely—he's a cultured man making a request. Klyucharyov can't, of course, refuse, he's embarrassed (he'd just thought something bad about him). On our darkening streets, you know, practically all the telephones are disconnected. But he'll try. He'll definitely try... No, it won't cost anything.

The warehouse. The row of locked doors. But one door is slightly open—Klyucharyov glances in, and there's dear Aunt Lyalya, that ageing curvy babe (when will he ever rid himself of the jargon of his youth), in her clean violet smock, still lying there as he had left her on the pile of resilient sacks. Klyucharyov enters—and starts to talk anxiously about material. From her reclining position, Lyalya gives a nod that she understands. "So I'm needed again!..." she laughs without getting up.

Klyucharyov, already accustomed to this, explains that he needs material that's water-repellent but also warm.

"We have some. Third storeroom."

She speaks lazily, scarcely raising her head. Still leaning back. Her eyes are moist and content; perhaps she'd dozed a bit but more likely she'd simply just not come down from that sweet moment. A proper lady. She looks at Klyucharyov with weary eyes, weighing whether she should sleep with him now or let it go this time.

The keys are right beside her and one of her hands limply plays with them (Music! They make a little jingle!). The keys lie on the checkered sack as if they, too, are exhausted by the music and she glides her fingers across them, making a soft ring which exactly corresponds to her tranquil emotional state. "Come closer. Closer. Please..." He stands beside her. She smiles. With the same hand she reaches—still reclining—toward his pants, which are just at the right height. She places her hand inside with the same laziness, and while looking him in the eyes, runs her fingers over him the way she'd just been playing with the bunch of keys. Klyucharyov keeps silent and her fingers glide over him. But apparently having decided that she's not in the mood or she's just too lazy to exert herself right now, she's content with the minor pleasure of arousing him—it's somewhere in between a caress and play. Then she twists into a little ball and wraps herself in an unfashionable warehouse blanket. "Take the keys," she says. She lies wrapped in the blanket with her legs drawn up and follows Klyucharyov with her eyes as he proceeds past the locked doors.

Material that had gone out of fashion (water-repellent and warm too, with a nap). Just the right colors–from gray to an earth brown. Behind the third door Klyucharyov painstakingly rummages through everything to pick a piece. And when he has chosen it, he rolls the piece of material up, trying to make the roll even, without creases.

He carries off two pieces of material that he has formed into narrow rolls. Two spears. (Two tied-up fishing rods.)

The well-preserved old woman is sleeping, and Klyucharyov (unexpectedly) senses his human compassion for her ageing, for her years. We all grow old. He places the keys beside her. "I'm not asleep," she says, apparently trying to excuse herself–she's sleeping and tries to express some feeling without having to open her sleepy eyes. "I'm not sleeping. I'm just drowsy..."

A poet stands on an outdoor stage, microphone in hand. His words make a slight echo. There's less light here, but more glow. In addition, two projector beams are fixed crosswise on the poet who's reading (when the poets switch places the projector lights also separate, one light following the person who's just performed, the second light picking out of the crowd whoever will be the next to read and taking that person to the microphone in an oval of light). All around people stand rooted in place listening, and Klyucharyov doesn't even try to work his way closer; with the rolls pressed to his chest, he stands some distance away, but he's also transfixed. Words have a power over him. He only vaguely perceives the poetry upon first hearing but from time to time talent will sparkle, and mystery, like a lake at morning, will rise in a white mist above the water of the spoken lines. Klyucharyov becomes intoxicated. The poet, in his opinion, has grown immensely. In size and art.

The gestures of his hands are measured, the artistry unquestionable, and even that certain loudness of breathing that is a tribute to the microphone doesn't matter.

Not far away there is a whole clutter of kiosks where small books of poetry for sale are on display. Good taste is being cultivated. Klyucharyov sees a young salesgirl who holds open a small volume and follows the lines of verse with her eyes while simultaneously listening to the author's performance (Nirvana?).

Klyucharyov also sees the poet who will follow the performer who's now on stage. He's a total wreck. His cheeks are flushed, he can't control himself... The verse ends with a wave of applause, noise, and cheers. Notes (questions) are passed to the front over people's heads. At the microphone the poet takes one after another. The white notes take wing and twist about like white butterflies in the intersecting lights.

Klyucharyov also sees death; right here, two steps away. While listening to the poems, a man began to cough, then doubled over. Whenever he seemed about to straighten up, he would double over again... until finally he collapsed with his head bent back. A young man. People say that death is taken lightly here. Some people glance over, but because of the public's preoccupation with the reading, almost no one notices. Still, people in white coats rush to the fallen man right away, and as soon as they've established that he's dead, they carry him off. It all goes quickly.

When a human or an animal dies suddenly, not only do their workhorse hearts break down, but all their muscles, including the bladder. And so a thin childish stream involuntarily dribbles out, the last release from the stress and responsibility of living. This excusable little spot remains on the pavement now—not far from Klyucharyov. Almost right in front of the kiosk with the young salesgirl holding the volume of poetry in her hands. But it seems to be common knowledge that the spot won't be absorbed, for two other people come now to scrub and wipe and sprinkle sand. Now all that can be seen on the pavement is a small dark oval the size of a palm—a child's palm. That's all that's left.

* * *

HE'S LOST. Klyucharyov had turned onto the street with the brightly lit grocery stores more or less at the right spot (the whole time he kept thinking that he'd forgotten about the tea, they needed a supply of it), but he'd have to find a shorter way back. There are hundreds of grocery stores, but what's the fastest way to get through them and back to the wine cellar with the hole? It's precisely this search for a short cut that leads to confusion: to a situation where one street (somehow so familiar and flooded with light) turns into another (which seems even more familiar!) and is marvelously lit but nonetheless leads to a square in which, Klyucharyov realizes, he is standing for the first time. He has managed to buy the tea, but now has to find his way out of here.

Once he understands that he has lost his bearings, Klyucharyov tries to figure out the right direction. He has to quicken his pace. For comfort's sake he puts the rolled-up material over his shoulder (a warrior with two spears) then off he goes.

He remembers that quite recently he'd been lost up there on the dark streets close to his home (here he'd been thrown off by the abundance of light and advertisements, while there it had been from the absence of lighting and by the darkness). On that dark street he'd only wanted to get hold of a candle. One can't live without candles, and Klyucharyov had even been ready to steal, in that new sense of the word "steal" that recently had sprung up and taken root, namely: to pick out something from the mess of stolen and senselessly scattered goods. Someone had broken into an enormous store window, both panes of glass were almost totally smashed. But even so, after giving the place a once-over, as is proper for a novice thief, Klyucharyov entered the store (he didn't crawl in, but simply walked in–so large was the hole in the window). He strode along past the depleted food section to the looted though not completely cleaned-out "Sundries" where there were jars of rouge, some lusterless tubes whose labels

Klyucharyov couldn't make out in the semidarkness, even toothpaste, but no soap and—oh no—not a single candle. It was then, precisely while searching for candles, that he'd wandered off to the loading docks, remembering rumors about some alleged freight cars that still hadn't been unloaded. He suddenly became lost in the midst of the train cars. He knew he was at the rear of the station and that he must be quite close to his home, but he couldn't find any way out at all. Just cars, cars, cars...

He'd seen several cars then that were filled with criminals who hadn't been deported yet from the city. He noted the pathetic system of guarding—two soldiers on every other car. The soldiers were quite young. They stood there, marking time in the semidarkness. They didn't even shout at Klyucharyov, who had come a little too close to them—they just looked, apparently waiting to see whether he'd say something to them. But what could he say?... As he was walking past, Klyucharyov heard a muffled din from the barred cars. People were stomping and banging inside. Loud curses could be heard. Somewhere, he thought, a board ripped off one of the cars was slowly creaking. Certainly the young soldiers were doomed, and perhaps for the first time in his life, Klyucharyov's heart didn't go out to the ones behind bars, but to those who were guarding them. The young soldiers wore tense smiles. They stood shivering in the evening air while trying to keep up each other's spirits with wisecracks. When Klyucharyov rounded the final car, one of the young soldiers couldn't stand it any longer and asked, "Do you happen to know if they're changing guards soon?"

No, Klyucharyov didn't know.

While walking around the train he'd spotted another dark mass of apparently empty cars. He had to walk around them, then turn and make his way slowly back to the station—there wasn't a spark of light anywhere! And so Klyucharyov strayed into the dark. The darkness between cars had weighed on his eyes then, and the glare of beckoning neon lights weighs upon him now.

Klyucharyov has already gotten his bearings, though. The street glitters and the dipping line of street lamps points the way. A lively group of people is walking toward him and, ah, there's a neon sign that Klyucharyov recognizes. He crosses to the other side (his mind still holding on to the memory of the recent past, so that at the same time he's now moving toward the station through the crush of hard dark cars. Aha! Klyucharyov sees the small dots of the signals, and he dives under a car and gets out on the other side of the train). Klyucharyov moves as if he's in two spaces at the same time, but inasmuch as they are one people and one land, why would it be so strange if both spaces coincided geographically—after all, Klyucharyov is travelling both here and there. And if he's lost, if he has gotten off track, then he is lost both here and there. In solidarity with his other street self. Klyucharyov walks between the book and newspaper kiosks and the lights of the advertisements pound so in his eyes that he crosses back to the other side of the street, where open doors beckon and people are chewing and drinking and the enticing smell of roast coffee is like no other smell in the world. (Congruent spaces. At the same time Klyucharyov is bending down and diving under the next dark car because he doesn't have enough strength to go around yet another long empty train on this tangle of rails. He sees small lights, then a large dark mass. Now there's puffing—it's a locomotive, probably a switching engine, then finally a living man is before him, a railroad worker with a dim lamp. He hits Klyucharyov's face with a ray of light—his way of asking, who do we have here?

"Go around the train and keep going straight. You'll end up right at the station," the railroader explains to the lost Klyucharyov.)

Congruent spaces. So it's not surprising that on the corner there's a man with a newspaper standing beneath a bright sign to whom he can turn with a question. The man is respectably dressed, and he answers the question calmly:

"Cross the street and keep going straight. You'll end up right at your restaurant once you pass the stores."

As he gives directions to the lost Klyucharyov, he folds up his paper for a minute and points out the direction with his hand—over there.

He doesn't have far to go now, and Klyucharyov decides to have a beer. He buys a bottle, finds a spot on a corner (even leaning a little against the wall to rest his legs), tips back his head and drinks the beer straight from the bottle. A marvelous forgotten pleasure. But Klyucharyov immediately tries to spoil his own pleasure, "It looks bad! Go to a cafe," he says and scolds himself for having carelessly tossed the bottle cap practically beneath a pedestrian's feet. He has remembered. He's guilty. But at the same time he'd been walking among the dark train cars. Some of them had bars on the windows. Muffled obscenities wafted from the cars. Klyucharyov was here, on the bright street, and he was there, next to an old car built out of planks, where smells of lubricating oil and old wheels hung in the air. There might not just be criminals in the cars; there might be people sentenced unjustly—his feelings are complex. Which explains Klyucharyov's gesture—the throwing of the bottle cap at the sleeping cars that smell of past decades. Caught unawares on this brilliant street, which glows with light, with a feeling of guilt he sees his beer cap on the lilac pavement, his hand tipping back the bottle and pouring the gurgling beer straight into his mouth. What is he doing? How could he be doing this?...

Klyucharyov comes to himself (totally finds his bearings in space) and goes off to finish his beer—he'd managed to take three or four gulps—in a cafe. He holds the bottle with a steady hand; as it loses strength, the bottle releases a heavy froth.

Klyucharyov doesn't forget his rolls of material either; he takes them along.

A CAFE-CLUB—that's the sort of cafe he finds. People are streaming in and Klyucharyov is drawn there too (in part it's still the aesthetic of the old train cars—the more people there are, the easier it is). But it turns out that there's a sociological survey taking place in the cafe (there are surveys here, wherever you go) which of all things in the world has to do with people's faith in the future. But what future do they mean? The immediate future?

There's too much talk about politics in this cafe for Klyucharyov's taste, but he's here already, and therefore he discreetly sits down with his bottle of beer at a small table. He orders some hot sausage and mashed potatoes to go with the beer—there isn't much money left, but he should fortify himself now.

There's a conversation at the next table. An age-old topic, of course. Perhaps these days it makes sense to like the mob in order to understand its concerns better, or perhaps there's no sense in considering the interests of the mob at all (they don't know what they want themselves!), and in that case the mob should simply be deceived. But should it be deceived for its own good?!

"Maybe we need a new idol," they reason. They're leaning over the table with their faces close together, but their voices are loud enough to be heard. "A man who doesn't flaunt his intellect, who's liked by the masses, if possible, a good man."

"But we had one of those! We had one!" some shouts interrupt. "In our time, however, this man must be liked. Have a new, a completely new image. Not a father-of-the-people image, but, let's say, the image of a great scholar who'll (with our help!) invent something in the field of economics to save us. Or how about the image of a simple practical man who can understand and forgive our weaknesses? Never mind—we can make him into a hero. Find wisdom in his simple remarks. We'll inflate him. Exalt him! But how can we know if he'll please the ordinary masses? The simple and insipid mob?..."

As they decide upon a representative type, they quickly flip through a card file of famous people from the past. Not only politicians are beloved. The first name is Nikon, who defeated the Old Believers. Then the venerable Leonardo. The smiling Alexander Pushkin. Zhukov, with his enormous chin. Chaplin, with his walking stick, but in terribly worn-out shoes—the look of poverty. Who'll emerge now, in our time, as the favorite of Her Majesty the Mob? And what if no pure prototype is found, if a hybrid is needed—then in what proportions and who's to be mixed with whom?... (Klyucharyov listens carefully. He orders another beer. The soft light of the cafe lamps plays on the full frothy head.)

A guy with a beard is searching for a more general alternative, "Maybe what we need now is not an idol but, on the contrary, someone people would openly hate, and since they would hate him they could take things out on this hated celebrity day after day. As a rule, people are dissatisfied with themselves. They have a lasting, if not eternal, dissatisfaction with themselves. And this is embodied in their dissatisfaction with *their* government, *their* empty store shelves, the fear of walking on *their* darkening streets... But whatever will we invent, what can we invent if people are persistently dissatisfied even when store windows are bright and the counters are full?!"

"Just a minute!" interrupts the man sitting across from the guy with the beard. "A person must still find his niche. A man is something concrete—don't inflate him. Don't make it 'either this—or that.' Either he'll find a niche for himself in the form of love for some image or super-image (and immediately become secluded in this love, as in a niche)—or everything will go to the devil. And don't, I beg you, don't make an enigma out of a man, don't make of him a giant!"

The conversation becomes heated, they're all talking at once now. "What? You think it's just about deceiving the mob with an image?! What? Our smart friend here thinks the whole problem is simply how to deceive the mob and the masses? Cheat them, huh? Let them be lulled by love for someone?..."

They've become overagitated. They're shouting. Klyucharyov doesn't trust the conversations of politicians—people who are in a hurry to live and a hurry to die. At high speed. With that intensity of the ambitious that destroys the psyche. (For them a conversation is a way to assert themselves. For them a wake is a way of earning points.) But he's not casting stones at them. And he's ready to believe them, if only they work for the good of the people. Every labor deserves gratitude, doesn't it? Isn't it also a spark of the divine? There comes a moment in impassioned political debates when the speakers hit a wall of exhaustion. As if they're stunned. They stop fighting, and in their silence one can feel the soundless vibration of the sublime words. (A minute from now they'll throw themselves at each other again, but this minute also is part of time—the time of unconscious brotherhood is brief.)

They're shouting too much. (But he's in a cafe, what can you expect?)

Passions are also heated in the adjacent small hall located in back of the cafe. That's where people constantly go, stay for a minute or two, and then leave. It's that very hall of *attitudes toward the future,* where the survey is taking place. The survey is extremely simple. If you believe in the future of your dim streets, you pick up your ticket at a small registrar's window and take it with you. If you don't believe, you return the ticket. (It's very straightforward. Returned tickets are thrown directly on the floor.) People in the cafe occasionally glance over at the growing heap of returned tickets. It's already quite large. And here comes someone else, a man or a woman, who adds another ticket to the pile of paper. Returning *a ticket to the future.*

There are several people in the hall from the polling commission but there's no longer even a trace of neutrality on their part. It's probably for this reason that passions have become so hot. They're trying to convince the people entering the hall to believe in the future; they explain, insist, practically push the tickets into their pockets. Even so, these people also throw down their tickets: there's been too much blood, you see, and too many tears have been shed, and so we don't believe in it, we have no desire for a future of blood and tears. We don't want it.

One member of the commission, who discarded all neutrality long ago, changes into an orator before everyone's eyes. He had been silent for a long time. A thin man, with burning cheeks (and looking incurably ill—Klyucharyov is ready to feel sorry for everyone), he starts shouting in a frenzied voice to the people who are leaving:

"Come to your senses! The future is your future! Haven't you been eating and drinking your whole life at the expense of someone else's tears and blood? Yes, no matter what kind of future there is, right now you're sleeping and eating and drinking at the expense of hundreds of thousands of children's tears, you're already dirty, you're branded! Take your tickets with you, become reconciled! Uphold what you learned in school and high school, at least, it's your, your—I won't tire of repeating it—your future! No matter how much you disown it now, no matter how you run from it after you leave..."

He's screaming. He's screaming in a frenzied voice. But they keep on throwing down their tickets, they are returning their tickets. The heap is already as tall as a man.

His haste has immediate repercussions: the bearded man rushes out of the cafe in pursuit of Klyucharyov, catches up to him, and right in the middle of the noisy street hands Klyucharyov the rolls of material he'd left behind. "I've been chasing you down the street like a guard with a spear!" he laughs, and Klyucharyov, who'd just remembered, thanks him.

5

The hole in the ceiling is large and ragged, but you can't tell if the gap has narrowed until you try pushing through. The ladder-stairway is in place, but there's something new—a square piece of canvas stretches beneath the hole, a special netting to keep the earth and stones that trickle down from falling on the tables where people drink and socialize. The net doesn't get in Klyucharyov's way at all. When

Klyucharyov climbs onto the top rung of the ladder with his purchases, he finds that he's already above the net.

Before making the climb, he has to arrange his simple gear. The rolls of material. The plastic bag with tea. The kerosene stove. Candles. What else?... While Klyucharyov is fiddling around, a conversation is taking place at a small table nearby. There are two young couples and an old man, and their conversation becomes so interesting that it catches Klyucharyov's attention; he doesn't want to leave yet—suddenly the warm comfort of companionship seems so dear to him, the cultivated style and the sublimity of words arising as if out of air. (The conversation and language seem to acquire sublimity and spirituality just when it's time to go.) Klyucharyov is already making an effort to concentrate: let's see, if I pull the rolls through the hole first, what will I do with the stove? "Yes, yes," they tell each other at the table, "It's clear! But how can we activate the features of individual personality that have been dissolved in the mob? The development of the individual today is still at the stage of sensory stimuli. It's almost biology." "But," one of the young women at the table argues impassionedly, "there's something besides the biological in man, but how can that *something* be stimulated. How?"

They talk. (Klyucharyov doesn't know the answer either. And he doesn't believe all that much in his idea about the cave. But if it's a matter of compatibility, then for the time being Klyucharyov will dig his cave, of course. And he can dig out another cave for his friend. He can dig one for his neighbor. But he can't widen the gap with his shovel: there's a limit here... Klyucharyov's thoughts turn more mundane. He notes to himself that the next time he'll have to buy a shovel with a short handle for work inside the cave.) They talk, "Can man be considered a creature capable of transforming life? Does man change life and himself? Or is he a creature who only wanders about restlessly because he hasn't yet found his true biological niche? Is that what mankind is: an enormous biological species searching for its niche, searching, to be sure, by trial and error and with its own limitations? We can't go this way.

And that way's impossible too. And consequently our limits are determined by can'ts. The tortoises have found a niche, the apes have found one, and we're still looking. Oh, how quickly we'll rest contented then! How satisfied we'll be with everything! When we find..."

They talk sincerely and with pain about the (quite modest) result of human development. Their sublime words are vague and not very convincing, but they're spoken with the hope that even approximately true sincere words will expand the soul (the gap in our soul), and the pain expelled from within will speak in words that are new. The words won't come as cries, they'll simply leap to mind of themselves, and maybe people will be silent when they have understood them: That's it! (And will the mob become good? Will the mob of thousands become good and completely unthreatening, peaceful on their way from the movies or from a large bounteous dinner party when the night is full of stars, and a voice in the crowd is singing?)

They talk and Klyucharyov brings up the rolls of material, the tea, and the stove to the top rung of the stairway... He feels connected to their words, they are dear to him. But man is finite. Man is mortal. And, as always, it's time to go, and it seems that the conversation has finally peaked...

They talk.

Klyucharyov has somehow squeezed himself into the gap. With his arm extended, he's shoving up his rolls of material and trying to push them up and out, not for the first, but for the third time now. A Cossack hitched a battle flag to his spear in roughly the same way—at the very peak, that is. Klyucharyov has hitched a bag with tea and candles to one roll and the package with the kerosene stove to the second. The additional attached load brushes against the side, knocking down earth and pebbles. While holding the roll in his extended right arm, he must push ahead almost to the neck and from there fling out the roll. Despite the difficulty he manages to heave out one roll on the third try, the other, on the fourth. Now Klyucharyov begins to climb out. He swallows the dust that's still swirling around in the hole from all the shoving, and his eyes are full of sand.

When he twists himself into the neck, Klyucharyov is conscious of the usual pain that accompanies each movement. This time the gap is bent in such a way that his head can only push through at an angle. His cheek bleeds from the scraping, it's like being skinned alive. Now the narrow spot. As always, Klyucharyov suffers a moment of stupor here, feeling the finality of being stuck, the loathsome numbness. He has become a plug. His body no longer hurts, no longer aches from the abrasions, so closely and exactly has it adapted to the twists of the gap in this narrow place. Klyucharyov has crawled in so far and the displaced earth has stuck so tightly to his body that he's no longer himself: he's part of the earth, a tightly, if not perfectly, fitting filling of flesh and blood. In some future time he won't be able to budge in this exact spot–Klyucharyov will die here, and when he's dead he'll remain a filling, a plug. He'll decompose, ever shrinking, and the earth will close around him, blocking openings of light with dust and sand, or simply contract (which the earth can do), so that after his death Klyucharyov can expect to remain at his post, while his bones, with their previous persistence, take possession of the hole until it's so compressed that the earth becomes their common grave. "Oh, come on...," Klyucharyov braces his mind.

Gradually the horror of being stuck passes if you don't jerk. By their own means, muscle tissues can redistribute the body substances they encompass; it's clear that not only man's experience but also that of the worm again (from the very beginning, everything is ours) have led to the slow and ingenious process whereby the body's energy reflows. The possibility of moving an arm is felt from within, then a shoulder is able to shift a little, and, finally, you can turn more easily and tear your bleeding cheek from the earth to which it has stuck. A little here. A little bit more. The head pushes through. The head has passed through the narrowest part, and now the shoulders take on the pain. It's a dull, extensive pain. Klyucharyov still keeps in reserve the thought with which he cheers himself when in the neck– the idea that the earth is like a woman, a young woman maybe, and he's a man performing the eternal male act. (Maybe the ground hasn't closed up, hasn't contracted completely yet, only because each time Klyucharyov pushes through he gets snagged here again.) He pushes forward, cheering himself with the idea that the pain is mutual, that the hole in the earth is also hurt when he jerks forward and scrapes his shoulders and cheeks so that they bleed. It hurts the earth too. It hurts it every time. Repeating this idea like an incantation, with a last difficult twist Klyucharyov frees his knees from the narrow neck. He's out! Sand sticks to his torn cheek and stings. His head is spinning, but it's out of the hole now, his head's above ground. He sees the grass. Klyucharyov breathes in the wind coming off the river.

When he has finished climbing out, he sits for some time, feeling completely weak and empty, without a single thought. Sometimes he makes a sudden soft moan or grunts as he slowly comes to himself.

It's gotten darker, of course. Still, it's light enough to see. A normal twilight. In any case, Klyucharyov makes out some abandoned boats down on the river. The boats are moored alongside the bank. They sit in place on the water. No one has been there for a long time. A pale light shines on the river.

As he quickly glances up, Klyucharyov's eyes virtually hit a ragged black patch in the midst of the green landscape: his cave has been wrecked... There's no mistaking it! As he gets closer he sees clearly that someone discovered the cave and smashed it, maybe simply out of spite that it had been dug. Two empty vodka bottles are lying on the grass nearby, there are footprints in the soft soil. They even tried to start a fire, to warm themselves on other people's ruins.

It's a sad moment. "But it doesn't matter," Klyucharyov thinks. It's sad. But it doesn't matter. He hadn't believed in his idea very much.

A dead crow hangs from the bird-cherry tree. They had killed it and hung it over the ruins as if to say, dig here and you'll be digging your own grave.

But Klyucharyov swallows the lump in his throat. He'll find something positive even in this. Well, he thinks, from biology and hatred they've progressed to concrete signs one can understand. This is already a sign. It's already the beginning of a dialogue. (Signs and gestures are followed by words–isn't that right?)

He looks for his tools. They're gone. Obviously, they took them. He pokes around in the grass with his hands–not there either. (Well, maybe they liked the tools. Maybe they needed them more. He doesn't want to think that they simply tossed the shovel, crowbar, and pickax into the bottom of the ravine.)

He knows he's tired. He's tired but he won't complain; that's the way he is.

Klyucharyov goes home. He goes along the dirt path at first, then takes the paved path slowly up the hill. Naturally, he carries his load with him–the rolls of material, the kerosene stove, the candles.

He has come to the first of the five-story apartments. There's a store here, and in the twilight Klyucharyov can see his own faint reflection in the dark windows. Strips of paper have been pasted crosswise on the glass window-panes to warn everyone that there's nothing left in this store, there's no reason to break the glass.

Not a soul on the street. The windows in the five-story buildings are all dark and covered by curtains. There's the window of his apartment.

Klyucharyov stops for a minute to arrange the load he's carrying in a slightly different way. His arms are numb and tired. He sits down on the ground and puts the kerosene stove in the plastic bag with the tea and candles. He rearranges things, packs them up, and suddenly the tiredness hits him, and with the tiredness comes a short dream. This happens sometimes.

As a rule these dreams are unpleasant and always about the same thing–the earth around the hole has contracted and closed, the gap is gone and he's cut off forever, left behind on the dark streets. (In the most excruciating dream the earth falls in on him as he's crawling through–

Klyucharyov is stuck in the hole, he suffocates and dies. If he's sleeping at home, he tosses and gasps and thrashes around until his wife wakes him, "Stop it! Stop!") His dream today is not as painful as the dream in which he's stuck, but it's terrible. The hole is gone. What trace remains is negligible. Klyucharyov bends over it, and, sticking his head in as far as he can, he shouts down to them. He yells out the first thing that comes to mind–how there aren't any candles or batteries and that it's quickly getting dark on the street, how they'd smashed in his cave and hung a dead crow above it. (Logic isn't necessary. For them any information will do; their giant computers will decode it.)

As in all of these dreams Klyucharyov must yell to them in an extremely loud voice. He shouts. Then he puts his ear to the ground. And from below through the narrow burrow and the compressed earth he hears the words:

"Keep speaking! Speak."

Keep giving them information, that is, something, anything, whatever you want–go on! And through the narrow burrow Klyucharyov shouts to them about the deserted streets and the mob of trampling people many thousands strong and the apartment buildings with thousands of dark windows.

He puts his ear to the hole again. And again from there, barely audible, comes:

"Speak! Speak!"

He shouts that the approaching dark is destroying the individual. That even thugs and thieves are afraid of the streets. He shouts about Denis. He shouts about the pocketful of bread they have left. About hunger. He shouts that the curtains make it dark all the time, even when there's light... His thoughts are becoming confused. Still, it's important that these things be said from here. Let their computer-decoders work on it and decipher not only the meaning of his words but the horror of this dream, his confession that he's not prepared. He's aware that this is a dream, but let them break down his condition into psychological factors, aberrations of thought, pure information and other components. They must understand his language, which was encoded one moment by a spasm and the next by an indistinct articulation, and which was distorted anyway because of the shouting down the hole (adding the acoustics of reverberating noise). They must decipher this and understand it—who else can, if not they.

And now their answer. Klyucharyov lets down a thin cord to them, which, in the proper sense, isn't a cord—it's a very sturdy fishing line which will hold up well and slide through without catching on anything. Klyucharyov holds the free end in his hands and now he can feel them grasp and attach something to it there. It must be their answer and advice. Yes, help. (You give to me—I give to you, it's the only possibility for a direct exchange of thought.) Klyucharyov hauls in and pulls out the line. Aha. A long object appears, a stick. In the approaching twilight Klyucharyov can't tell what it is at first. Even less does he understand its meaning. His brain is weak after the lengthy continuous shouting. After the first stick another stick appears. Now Klyucharyov can see and he gropes for the curved end by which every stick is fastened to the line. For some reason Klyucharyov (it's a dream, after all) had expected to pull out a tightly scrolled text or some text on microfilm (something like those tubes of bamboo in which pilgrims smuggled out cocoons and the secret of silk from the Chinese), but there are no texts, there's not a single word in reply. He would have been glad if, at worst, they'd sent help in the form of candles, thin meter-long candles—could his information on the approaching darkness really have been unintelligible (garbled by his shouts?). Klyucharyov is too much an intellectual, and he would certainly have been a bit offended, he would have been irritated. Still, he would have been satisfied (there's no room for touchiness when hunger is everywhere) if instead of a reply directed to his mind he had just hauled in some small links of sausage on the line—they're so easy to pull. But no. He pulls out another stick with a curved end. And another stick. And another. But there's got to be some reply and Klyucharyov waits with definite, though not great, hope. Klyucharyov is pulling and pulling on a long, unending line and sticks are crawling out of the constricted hole one after another, and no matter how weak his brain might have become, Klyucharyov suddenly understands—*they are canes for the blind.* When total dark falls, you can keep on walking, tapping the sidewalk with your cane. This is their answer.

Klyucharyov keeps pulling and pulling, he has already pulled out hundreds, he has pulled out thousands of canes for the blind—and at last he wakes up. A terrible dream. And unjust, in Klyucharyov's view, in its real lack of trust in reason.

A GOOD MAN IN THE TWILIGHT. (So few and so many.) He had woken Klyucharyov, this passerby. Klyucharyov woke up near that same five-story building at whose corner he had rested and fallen asleep while repacking his candles and tea. He had slept for four or five minutes.

He heard a voice:

"Why have you fallen asleep?" A simple voice. "You shouldn't sleep on the street."

Still somewhat sleepy, Klyucharyov looks up. A man stands there. Middle-aged, with rather long hair that falls loosely, almost to his shoulders. Yes, he was passing by. He saw Klyucharyov sleeping and he woke him up.

"Get up," he repeats just as firmly, with a calm and patient smile. "You shouldn't be sleeping on the street."

He extends his hand. Klyucharyov would have gotten up by himself, and this man gives him only a little help. His hand is warm and his touch will remain with Klyucharyov even later.

Klyucharyov rises.

"Yes," he says, stretching. "It's gotten so dark."

"But it's not night yet," the man says, again with a soft smile, which Klyucharyov doesn't see as much as sense in the semidarkness.

Klyucharyov gathers his things and walks toward his home, which isn't very far now. He takes a look back. The man is still standing in the same place, and only as

Klyucharyov begins to walk away does his figure in turn ever so slowly dissolve (though not completely) in the twilight.

The Long Road Ahead

1

True, it's been two hundred years or so since we've had any wars, large or small, nations and corporations live in mutual trust, and humanitarian ideals have triumphed, but there's still a devilish secretiveness when it comes to research and development! It's cutthroat competition, and they really rip each other apart, damn them!—a young man thought as he got ready for a trip. He shaved carefully. He looked at himself in the mirror. "Sh-hhh!" he put his finger meaningfully to his lips.

They'd told him to get ready for a remote assignment and not to advertise it too much. All right, he promised, with a snort. He even grumbled. To be honest, the words of his supervisor had pleased him (as did the bit of mystery in the situation). It meant they valued him. That something important was going on. He became excited. And why shouldn't he? It was life, and he was a young man, working in Moscow, talented, ambitious, and about to fly off on a mission to a proving ground located somewhere in the southern steppes. He would fly there as the inventor of his own—yes, his!—assembly, the ATm-241, and he was ready to install it, full of confidence and a good measure of vanity, just about right for a young man.

He took a plane to one of the provincial cities, and from there flew to the proving ground on a special helicopter—and as its sole passenger. Official secrets and competitive wars among enterprises were too much in vogue, but some day competition would become superfluous, and they'd get rid of all these spies and superspies, all these loafers! the young man mused (strictly speaking, he was experiencing the secretiveness as just loneliness right now—there wasn't anyone to talk to!).

The success of the ATm-241 belonged to him and his co-workers—they'd all be rewarded. One way or another the feedback would lead to recognition. Would success result in an expansion of the division? He didn't know; and he didn't want to run mentally ahead—the anticipation itself was pleasant. Society would remember him, that was certain. But the most important thing was the creative satisfaction he would get when his work was recognized! Naturally he wanted fame—he was young.

And being a young man, he experienced a certain state of excitement simply from the very fact of the trip: leaving the usual rut for something unfamiliar predisposed him, perhaps, to seek adventure, or perhaps (through genetic memory) it simply resurrected in him a young man of distant times who lived in a state of heightened readiness. Whatever the cause, as soon as he climbed out of the helicopter he had an intimation of a sensual explosion, and it suddenly occurred to him that maybe he expected to meet a woman—yes, yes, that was it! Owing to the secrecy in this part of the world, people are a bit isolated here, and the local women, for instance, had to be old-fashioned and inexperienced in matters of sex (this excited him!), and then there was that marvelous antiquated manner of speaking—who knows, any journey to unknown places is like a birth. A man must begin, as it were, from the beginning, and there can't be any beginning without an encounter or without a woman, without Adam and Eve—let it be just an approximate and proximate variant—the young man mused, not only sensing an understandable surge of strength in himself as he faced the new, but feeling his heart pleasantly skip a beat as well. At the same time his manner remained calm and correct—this was a business trip.

A sturdy jeep in a protective color and with tarpaulin sides drove up to the helicopter.

The young man told the man who met him, "Why? I don't have any luggage. And I can see it's right over there."

And that was true, the manufacturing plant and proving ground was close by, about a kilometer, and in such weather and with the steppe so splendid he wanted to walk that kilometer, to hear the grass crunch underfoot and stretch his muscles after sitting cramped in the airplane. Everything on the steppe could be seen exceptionally well—the protectively colored wall around the plant was clearly visible, distinct supporting pillars setting off the gray span of wall between them. It was beautiful precisely in its grayness and its ordinary appearance, which was so natural in the steppe, yet to which his eye was unaccustomed, having been exhausted by the bright colors of the big city. They insisted that he ride, anyway. The hypnotic effect of travel. The people meeting him even wanted to take his bag. "No, no. I'll take it! Really, the bag's very light!" And he jumped, rather than climbed in–jumped lightly into the jeep, full of energy. At the plant, of course, the steppe would no longer be the same. Oh, it was too fast! But the wind with its smells of wormwood and wild hemp swept through the openings in the tarpaulin–take a deep breath!–swept in and blew across his face, and the steppe was there, the steppe was beside him, the steppe had not yet ended, and at last he had a sensation of arrival. "Only three days," he thought regretfully, and one of the people who had greeted him and sat down beside him said, as if he'd caught the thought when it splashed out, "You'll be here three days!" But he spoke with a different intonation: you'll have to manage somehow and just be patient if you're suddenly faced with everyday inconveniences that you wouldn't find in the big city.

But, of course, it was understood that this was only a manner of speaking, that they'd take care of him and there wouldn't be any inconveniences.

The wall was getting closer now, he was able to examine it. Brick, painted with gray paint that was chipping. He saw a wall that stretched straight ahead and went on and on. At first glance the wall didn't give an impression of severity and surveillance, though its inconspicuousness, the chipping paint and the expanse that had evidently been cleared in all directions spoke precisely of scrutiny. Of an eye. Of the fact that no one would approach it, take an interest in why the wall was chipping or ask why no one painted it. A wall that was a real wall. The gate came into view. When they were even closer, they saw before them, forming an arch above the gate, an equally inconspicuous inscription, of the sort found in all places closed to outsiders: "WELCOME."

It was a small house. An elegant one. A dacha on a small lot with a garden, he said to himself. Yes, very nice. And there's another one just over there. Two in all. Not many people come here, it seems. I do know how to count. People come here rarely and only by themselves, two at the most.

"You'll be by yourself here," his escort said. Their thoughts ran parallel, they were obvious thoughts. "You might be a bit bored..."

"I like being alone," the young man smiled in reply.

They went inside. His dacha, as he called it, was small, but neat and well kept. Three rooms, rugs. A nice desk with a set of pens. A computer, naturally. A sparkling bathroom–his escort flung open the door, as if to say, take a look, admire it.

"The little house nearby is also a guest house, it's empty for the time being, and in that building farther off is the company commissary. You can order your food there. Don't think our daily fare is bad, on the contrary. You're young and probably have a healthy stomach, but if there's a special diet you want prepared, they'll do it–they've thought of everything here. There's only one cook, but he's an expert. You can eat unsalted food, for instance, and not even know it."

His escort took a step toward the door.

Then he stopped, "I'll say good-bye for now. Take a rest. You'll work tomorrow. Someone will come by for you at nine in the morning... And you should really decide about your diet today, even if you don't feel like eating after your trip. The cook should know your weaknesses. I'm joking, of course..."

He was at the door when he shouted, "The refrigerator is stocked with wine and juices!"

The jeep with the tarpaulin sides started up and drove away.

So, he'd gotten a first-class welcome. And why not? The plant produced the highest grade of synthetic protein, which is then processed into the food that feeds us all. That's why the technology is kept secret, not just because of government regulations, but also because the competition is tough. The number one problem is protein. The beef or pork, let's say, is created synthetically on the basis of models from centuries ago. (It's been almost a hundred years since fish or fowl or anything living has been used in food–that's humanism!) We know for a fact that only grasses are used, but the rest of the process, sorry to say, is a secret. There are many manufacturing plants, and apparently they've been scattered cleverly here in the steppe–there's grass and more grass all over the place and enormous enclosed areas of steppe. And how could they help but give a fine welcome to the person who'd brought such a thing as the ATm-241 to their conservative world?

His thoughts flowed easily, even somewhat exuberantly. In the meantime he looked the place over, getting used to the walls and to the prints that had been hung with old-fashioned obtrusiveness on the blank areas of the walls. The relentless whiteness of the day. Something grew tense in him again, as if preparing for danger, in expectation of something. He caught himself repeating a thought, and took note: that's it, the memory of the young man from times past who had to run well, like a young wolf, in order to survive. He smiled, amazed at the tenacity of genetic memory. Every now and then the past comes to life. You make a move in space and it's like moving in time. It's amazing!

Before going to sleep he took a short walk in the vicinity of his house, circled around it, and breathed in the air from the steppe.

* * *

They set off in twos for the factory buildings.

"...We don't need your theoretical stuff. You're wasting people's money, and how! Besides, all of these innovations of yours naturally result in information leaks. You come here–and then you'll go, won't you? In the past things were completely different. If someone installed something for us, he'd stay on. Forever. That's the only way. If you love science, devote your life to it–then we'll believe in you and your love. You think you've helped us? How can you help from there? We've managed without you till now, don't you think we'll manage after you leave?"

The young man on assignment understood that there was nothing unusual about the old engineer's grumbling (it was typical even, dedicated old-time workers are supposed to grumble), but still he remarked, "But I have worked–I've been thinking about the problem for several years. Why do you treat my work with such indifference?"

Pops (as the old engineer was known here) quickly shot back, "That's just what I was saying. Why should a man be uprooted? Let him go on sitting up there in the city thinking as much as he wants..."

"Listen, that's insulting. Why did I work so hard then? Why should people work hard at all?"

He was insulted, and even felt a spasm in his stomach–how unpleasant. He kept very quiet and tried to suppress the insult, but he sensed the stomach tension wouldn't go away. And only then did he realize that the unpleasant feeling wasn't coming from something inside–it came from outside. That smell. What was it?...

"Don't look around. Don't poke your nose into things. You'll see everything, but in strict order–when your assembly's turned on."

Old people are as bound by rules as ever, that's clear. The young man scanned the conveyor line. The smell came from the five or six vats that hung rather high above them and were slowly moving ahead. The smell stabbed his nostrils, penetrating to his soul, and the young man knew it at once—the smell of synthesized blood. In order to synthesize meat it's necessary to synthesize blood too. But the smell was searing, something had gone wrong with the chemical composition...

"Is it too strong? Take a sip," Pops said, offering him a bottle.

"I don't need your liquor. I'm not a kid," the young man said, and he pushed away the hand with the bottle that the old engineer had stuck right in front of his nose, maybe hoping to hide the smell.

But perhaps the synthesis hadn't been bad. Maybe this was even a sign of quality—the smell of blood is known to evoke aggressiveness, and I might be under its influence now, the young man thought.

"Pay attention," Pops's grumpy voice rasped again. "This is the terminal point. The completely finished product (he didn't say *meat*) exits here and you see the clock there. It shows the time of processing from the moment the knife switch is turned on. The exact time... Your assembly modification must not increase the whole processing time by more than forty seconds. I know, I know. Don't interrupt! I know that you've set a time loss of twenty-six seconds. But I take the liberty of strongly doubting that. Let it be forty seconds! I don't care! However, if there's a loss of more than a minute, I'll go on my own to the director of the plant and ask him to throw you out of here and file such a *complaint* against you to your organization that they'll clip your wings once and for all in the place where you, excuse the expression, work so hard! It will haunt you for the next ten years, understand?"

"Yes."

"No, you don't understand! I'm an old engineer and I know what it means to stop the conveyor. What it means to interrupt the cycle. And because of you we're stopping the line for almost a minute while we mount your ATm-241..."

He motioned to him, "This way."

They went outside (they'd walked all the way through the last conveyor room with the hanging clock). It was easier to breathe now, the air was fresh, and you could feel the nearness of the steppe. In the distance stood two-story orange houses, attractively set behind a high wall of green vines, wild grapes, maybe, or hops?

Pops explained, "Our workers live there. And, in order to prevent information from leaking out, they never leave. They don't even want to leave. We have excellent stores here, nice outfits for the women, the latest styles. And a great sports center with swimming pools! Why the wall around the plant buildings? No special reason. Just so our kids don't run in here if they're chasing some bright butterfly. So the smells don't get to their souls..."

"Are we waiting for someone?"

"Your technician's on the way. Anyway, we can't be too secret here, of course; neighbors will be neighbors, and a family's just that—everyone knows everything. And we don't forbid anything, of course, we simply advise people to leave the cows out of their family conversations," Pops nodded his head in the direction of the vats, "it's better that way. 'Cow' is a nice word, but we advise against using it."

The young man looked up at the line of vats slowly sailing by. In shape they really did resemble cows that were slowly moving ahead one after another toward some habitual watering hole. The technical engineer arrived (the man who'd already built the ATm-241 here from the sketches and diagrams the young man had sent ahead), introduced himself and shook hands energetically. The ATm-241, which the young man had spent so much time conceiving and the technical engineer so much time building with his own hands, had bound them like twins. Like friends who've supported each other for many years. They looked at each other with curiosity, as if feeling a distant kinship not based on blood.

"Our old man's grumbling again, is he?" the technical engineer winked at the man on assignment—he obviously had Pops in mind. But he mellowed at once. "Don't pay any attention. He's a good man, he really has a great big heart, our Pops!"

He tried to give the old engineer a friendly pat on the back, but Pops pushed his hand aside: "What next?... We've got work to do, this is no party."

They fixed a time to meet and the technical engineer left.

The conveyor slowly rolled out the cow-vats. Women dressed in white worked near the vats, pushing in knobs and shooting out exact doses of flavoring additives from their ampules. The women were young and the white clothing accentuated the shape of their bodies. Suddenly another wave of smells passed, he felt sick again, and in the midst of nausea his manhood was aroused. Instinct, the young man on assignment told himself, observing that no matter how repulsive the smell was, it gave a man a sense of strength, even power. He stared at the female bodies in their white clothes. He picked out one and imagined what she was like beneath the uniform.

"Why'd they do such a bad job sealing the vats?" Pops muttered angrily. He brandished the bottle again. "Don't you want some? A sip or two? Well, thank God you don't want it. The smells affect people differently, someone who's not used to it can even get hysterical. One man–he was standing right where you're standing–started to tear out that railing there, see it?–with his hands; he shook it back and forth trying to steady his nerves. And so he bent it, of course. See there? He bent the metal, and he seemed like such a puny intellectual..."

Pops started to hurry–let's get out of here fast! (He took a swig from his bottle.)

They went back through the building, walking against the direction of the conveyor line.

"...I saw how you looked at that woman–there's an example for you. For ages the act of procreation wasn't discussed openly, it was a carefully guarded secret. The act was shrouded in love and feeling, and not only in churches of all denominations, but also in the world at large. And why?... Because no one had ever perfected procreation. But as soon as abortions, pills, and hormones made their appearance, as soon as men began stuffing a night's supply of rubbers in their pockets, excuse me, I meant to say prophylactics, I'm just an old man, please excuse me—and, after all, this was still long before we succeeded in conquering AIDS, and AIDS was conquered only in the last century!—then everything was all out in the open, no more secrets! Now even snotty teenagers—I heard this yesterday with my old ears—say that the first time a woman goes with any man she's supposed to start moaning in bed so that he won't lose his self-confidence and potency, God forbid..."

"Excuse me. Are you talking about secrets?... Or about women?" he asked with a smile.

"Secrets, about secrets! What else would we be talking about? I've always argued against innovations of any kind, any sort of ATm-two hundred and forty lousy numbers... Now I just grumble, unfortunately, but earlier I was still able to persuade people. Just five years ago I convinced one young man not to install anything new. They'd sent him here, just like you, but I could convince him, and he refused to install anything and left..."

"That won't happen with me."

"Yes, I see. I can see that. But I did convince him. And he wrote in his report: I do not want to work with you... Unfortunately, there isn't any other kind of work for him in this world. Nothing that's been invented yet. So he left without having accomplished anything, poor fellow."

This old ninny, this grumbling Virgil of a Pops went on explaining things. "And here's the clock. See it? We'll be passing through here, too, when your ATm-241 is linked up to the conveyor. I'm a man of few words when an assembly is on a test run. I've got two words: *perfect,* and the second one is silence. You can figure out what that means. It means it's *crap.* And *perfect,* well, of course, that's if it keeps to the schedule you promised us and only forty seconds are lost. I know, I know about the twenty-six seconds! But who believes that? I'd like to spit on your millimicron laser method—I don't believe in it. I believe in lasers and in your ability to count, but I don't believe in the conveyor when it's made to go fast–it's sensitive, it has a life of its own, you can't just let it race!"

But a moment later a warm wave of emotion swept over him when the hellish Pops, without even a pause, announced, "Your assembly will be installed here. Here in this room. You can go in for a second..."

The room was medium-sized and completely empty. Only a transparent plastic hose stretched across the floor in the center of the room. Through the hose–you could see it clearly–a pulsating mash of future food pushed ahead in spurts. An empty room, and in the middle, a thin thread of hose. The young man on assignment was so overcome by excitement that he couldn't speak. A sign of deep feeling. His heart beat quietly, pumping out blood with nearly the same pulsating throbs. The transparent hose was breathing in and out like a blood vessel, and it was narrow–no thicker than a little girl's wrist. "So, they'll cut the hose here with a scalpel and within an hour your assembly will be installed and connected. The hose will feed into the ATm-241 and then lead out of it, of course. That's it."

The young man on assignment immediately set a condition–he wanted to watch the whole conveyor process while the test was underway. He wanted to be sure that seconds weren't lost somewhere at other junctions along the line.

"The overall time?" Pops asked with a nod. "Naturally, we'll take everything into account. But why do you care? Oh, you don't trust us. All right, you can look it over from start to finish, but only on the third day, the final one. You can track every second yourself. As you wish. You'll even get two chronometers. One you'll hold in your hand and maneuver back and forth, and the other, the one that's linked to the central computer, you can attach firmly to your gut–then you'll be free to look around."

Then he raised his brows, as if in warning, "You'll have two chronometers, all right, but I'll have two myself!"

"That's just wonderful," the young man grinned.

"Exactly. Wonderful. Two for you and two for me. There's even a chance the plant director will come with us for the conveyor part. But it's not definite."

* * *

She knocked softly, with a timid, old-fashioned tap, and when he said "Come in," she entered with a certain hesitation. In her hands she held an attractive small pail for the trash and a mini vacuum. A small radio phone, just slightly smaller than the palm of her hand, hung like a medallion from her slender neck. It must be for two-way communication; the administration could check where she was cleaning and the condition of the guest house at any time. She cleaned the rooms quickly and competently, pushing her dark hair off her forehead from time to time. She'd stop, then start to move again, stop and move. He stood by the window still reflecting on that emotionally confusing moment when she'd walked in shyly and quickly introduced herself, "Olya."

And he gave his name.

She was tidying a more or less clean room–brushing away thin layers of dust. After five minutes she washed her hands, took a look in the mirror and brought a tray with tea and a few pastries to the table. And he, naturally, said, "Stay with me a while. Have some tea with me." She sat down across from him, on the armchair.

They were both smiling–they could relax. They drank tea and talked.

"I was afraid you'd be old. Older men won't leave you alone..."

"And young men?"

She laughed, "And young men are embarrassed."

"Like me, you mean?"

She nodded and mumbled something he didn't catch. He noticed she was also embarrassed.

He said that probably no one had come to see them here for a long time.

"That's right. More than half a year..."

And quickly added, "Yesterday I saw your light on here. I was cleaning in the house next door. And I thought about you."

"Ah, so you were the one there. I saw a light in the windows, too; it was on for about three or four minutes, right?"

He sensed a mutual attraction, which at the moment was restrained and cautious, but which demanded action of some kind if it were to continue. Her face was somewhat plain, but attractive... He kept on talking, playfully, it seemed, and perhaps he was even a bit crude, but it was precisely because of his excitement, his confused feelings, that he fell into a strange kind of speech. The same thing seemed to happen to her–all at once a quick shy giggle burst out, and she immediately became embarrassed.

He turned on music after tea. Quiet music. Then he asked if she was married, and she answered "no," and at the same time shook her head–no. She stood up to go, and her face was flushed. He knew that in one more moment she would be gone. He quickly shut off the music on the tape player and walked toward her.

"You're so..." he started, but she put a finger to her lips, then pointed with the same finger to the little radio phone that hung close to her shirt pocket.

He understood. He nodded, as if to say, I'll be as still as a mouse.

He was confident now and held out his hands. She took a hesitant step forward. He even shut his eyes, like a teenager. "What happiness!" he thought and gasped for breath. And an hour later, after she'd gone, he repeated it to himself–what luck, what happiness, how happily I'll sleep now.

He was already in bed when he remembered that he was supposed to call the technical engineer if he hadn't heard from him.

"Excuse me," he spoke into the phone, "is it too late, were you sleeping? I'm just very jittery. Our assembly's being installed tomorrow. Did you look at it again today?"

"Of course I did."

"Hmm... Well, actually, that was my question. The only thing I wanted to ask."

The technical engineer laughed, "OK, don't be nervous now. Pleasant dreams. The assembly is a marvel. It's a real beaut!"

In his laughter there was not only cheer and the desire to impart cheer, but there was confidence. (Which is better than blind trust.) So the young man on assignment could also laugh now with relief. He hung up the receiver. And remembered that he could fall asleep happily tonight.

And at just this moment Olya came back. Her return was a surprise. She said something to him, she wasn't sure, she said, that the small refrigerator with the snacks was working... She stood on the threshold. The young man understood that she wanted to be with him, that she wanted to stay, but his face still openly expressed astonishment at the unexpectedness of her return.

"Don't be afraid. I won't stay," she said with a suggestion of humiliation.

"I'm not afraid of that. I want you to. I was just a little confused," he confessed truthfully.

It turned out she wanted to tell him something about herself, to share something. Yes, of course. Sometimes people just want to talk. They were lying side by side. Their love was unhurried now. She hardly made a noise, but this time was nicer than the first, the fever had run its course and was gone. A stage of pleasure closer to night than to evening. She was saying something about herself, telling a naive and simple story about how she'd lived somewhere in the Ukraine before. There were sunflowers, and the birds would fly up to them and peck at the large drooping heads. They'd wind gauze around the heads of the sunflowers, but the birds would still peck away their share. She didn't feel at all sorry for the sunflowers. The birds only came at sunrise when she, little Olya, was sleeping. And she'd had a terrible illness then.

"What was it?"

"I don't know."

"What were the symptoms?"

"I couldn't understand things well, I was slow. And I'm still like that. I learned almost nothing in school. I couldn't work anywhere..."

"But you should have been given disability benefits."

"I was. But I wanted to be with people. I wanted to work, but no one hired me... Finally they brought me here."

"Without the right to leave?" he asked.

"Yes."

She said that she'd gotten used to living here, and here, at least, she was living with other people. But sometimes she longed to go to the Ukraine. She longed to find that little house where she lay sick and could see sunflowers and hollyhocks from the window.

"Was it in early childhood, then?"

"M-maybe," she said, not remembering exactly and apparently being very careful about what she said, while at the same time doubting her own words.

He got up and walked in the dark to the refrigerator. He took the wine bottle and poured himself a glass. "Would you like some wine?" he asked. "Just a very little," she said. "Wine makes me completely stupid. I told you—I was sick and can't think well..." He drank, but she just held onto her glass and with the other hand covered her breasts with the sheet. Finally, she just put the glass down on the stand.

She said that she longed for the Ukraine and started to cry. Her heart even hurt, right here. "Put your hand here," she said. "Now here..." She was laughing quietly and bashfully: tee-hee, hee-hee.

2

The entire ATm-241 was in the room now: its parts were scattered on pieces of soft striped padding that looked like throw rugs. Two workers brought in the measuring devices (the assembling would also be monitored). While they were industriously bustling back and forth, the young man on assignment examined his creation in living form, for the first time, rather than on the drawing board or as a model on a test stand–it was made of metal and plastic, and the transparent drives stretched out in a row, one after another, spick and span, the protective coat of grease having already been removed. The technical engineer, well rested and in a good mood, was directing the preparations with his usual energy and cheer. He smiled and nodded to the man on assignment, as if to say, "Everything's OK!"

"That goes here! Put that over there! Put the second drive right here; yes, that's right, together with the base!" he instructed the workers.

Pops appeared.

"Good morning... Well, do you like the way our technical engineer works?"

"Very much!"

"You bet! He's one of our best specialists. Held in high esteem. One of the volunteers. Those who decided to work here the rest of their lives. To be honest, I'm fed up with the recruits and people sent on special assignment–please excuse an old man, but to me you're all just trash... We have to hide everything from you, cover it up, and waste a lot of good money at the same time."

The young man laughed.

"So it seems. You've done a great job of imposing secrecy. Just like they did in the past!"

"You think it's funny. But I get bad sleep from all this hide-and-seek and blind man's buff... Speaking of that, step over there to the guy with the mustache–we need to sign the secrecy agreement."

"Just a minute..."

While they were talking, the young man on assignment had been carefully examining each component of his assembly that had been brought in. Suddenly his eye fixed on something, his face turned red and he rushed over to a tall, thickset worker, "Put it down! Put it down!" He tore the packing foil away with his hands and studied the metal–he didn't like it. Instead of chrome-plated steel it was a dull whitish color—surely it couldn't be cheap material?! The technical engineer came over at once. They both crouched down over the connecting part. "Oh! Did that scare you? It's our Matte-metal!" The technical engineer tapped with his finger along the oval metal edge and the young man on assignment immediately heard the characteristic clang.

"Thank God!" he sighed with relief.

"What did you think? We wouldn't skimp on that!" said the technical engineer, and the workers nearby laughed in approval.

The man sent on assignment turned back to Pops.

"I'm coming!" he told the man with the mustache who stood there holding the agreement. On top of his large folder was the unsigned form and a fountain pen. The cap had even been removed and the tip smelled of india ink.

"No, they don't skimp on things. They're rich. The more secretive the organization, the richer it is—it's been that way forever and still is...," he thought, while his eyes skimmed the text. A standard legal text, but the consequences were severe. In the event a term is violated, in the event of the smallest information leak, the company may appropriate the ATm-241, the author loses all rights, the work commissioned from him is considered null and void; in virtue of its right to self-protection the company may also demand to have the author declared not of sound mind, and do so not only to ensure that the ATm-241 will become the sole property of the company in perpetuity, but also in order to discredit all information divulged by the author. The company has the right to ask the court to have the author declared mentally ill, with all the ensuing consequences, which the company is permitted to monitor, using all its resources and financial means. "Riches," he thought, as he signed it.

The technical engineer continued to direct the preparations, shouting out orders to the workers. The transparent hose-vessel with the pulsating mash still lay quietly in the center of the room.

"Do you see that?"

"I see it."

"So-o. We'll make a cut somewhere here and then–it's on its way..."

Pops put his arm around the young man's shoulder.

"I'm an old grouch, but, to tell the truth, I'm pleased with your assembly. It reduces the smell considerably, and in only forty seconds! I know, I know, twenty-six..."

The man on assignment had been prepared (this was to become clear on its own); and they'd led him to believe that during the process of installation each tiny step required a colossal effort.

"My assembly's extracting two amino acids from this mash just so that the product will smell better?"

"Yes."

"And I've used all my know-how, all my hard work just to make something smell less?"

"You really didn't know?"

"Yes, I knew, of course I knew!" laughed the man on assignment. "That's the usual way an idea finds it way to earth."

Pops began to praise him. "You have such wonderful filters. When an animal's slaughtered, it secretes trace elements of poison, in addition to adrenaline, which we know to be the hormone that helps creatures under attack defend themselves. Your filters will aid in removing some of it, they'll help refine the product."

"You make synthetic beef so well that you've learned to duplicate the trace elements of slaughter–ah, that's right, you're copying beef from centuries ago! Can't you depart from the model?! If the ATm-241 is but a grain of sand, just think what tremendous technological power your plant has!"

He was genuinely excited, but Pops interrupted him:

"Just a minute. They're calling you."

Indeed. He was being given a sign by the technical engineer, who held a plate with transducers in one hand.

The man on assignment went over–yes, the fourth purification tank with the magnetic filters, extraction at a low speed. The purification tank works on a flicker principle, and if a moment of flickering coincides with a moment of pulsation, the first input second can be lost. "That second doesn't count. That second's *their* second," he told the technical engineer. The engineer cracked a smile, relaxed, and said if that was the case he'd take a section of the hose, put it against the wall of the room, and let it work there.

The man on assignment now kept his eyes fixed steadily on the installation. He was constantly squatting down to check something (sometimes the technical engineer was able to push a small stool under him). It's amazing when your ideas have taken on a physical form–it's easy, painless work! The assembly seemed to have come alive already, the laser synchronizers were waiting to drive the protein mash through the transparent elastic sides of the new vessels.

"But here," Pops's voice could be heard, "we'll make an additional check."

Of course: it was in *their* interest to determine the fat content to the hundredth part. Without stopping the system for even a second, they'd extract a tiny sample of synthesized albuminous sausage, perform an instant microanalysis, then the computer would process the data and it would be sent back into the system. The refinement, clearly, lay in the fact that the sample would be taken *before* his Atm-241, but the data would go into the system on the next conveyor, that is, immediately *after* his assembly.

"Yes, go ahead, for God's sake," the young man on assignment replied with apparent willingness, and then casually asked, "What feeds into the monitoring device?"

Pops and the technical engineer made motions with their hands, "It's supplied from the conveyor! From the central conveyor, naturally! But that doesn't make any difference... One or two watts! It's nothing!"

The young man agreed, but then added, "Count it, all the same–is it one watt or two watts?"

They assured him that the general expenditure of energy would be figured in. The ten rooms that already had assemblies and now his room, the eleventh, all process the albuminous sausage until it meets the norm. The rooms and assemblies within them are reminiscent of the large and small intestines of the bowels, where fats are broken up in order to put less strain on the liver–of any person, but above all, of someone who might be living on a special diet. The pieces of meat would be synthesized in other rooms. But in order to remove the odor, they would go through his assembly.

They showed him through the glass how pieces of meat were forced along; sometimes they stuck sideways, but the advancing fluid would push them again, and with the next throb of the internal pulse the piece would break apart and (looking wonderful, tasty, and freshly cut, just begging for a frying pan or oven) crawl along on its way.

"Everything's terrific," the young man on assignment said.

"Hmmm..." from Pops. "You bet!"

"The only thing in the room that still puzzles me," continued the man on assignment, "is that box in the corner. It's not even unpacked. What's in it?"

Pops hemmed again, but in a different tone, "Hmm. Can't tell you just now. The box... a bit later on."

The man on assignment knew how to exert his will, however. He stood his ground–this was unacceptable. Could things just be brought into the room like that? An installation was taking place here. And he was responsible for the whole assembly.

"Just don't get so upset now," Pops rasped. "It won't be connected to your system in any way. That," he said quietly, "is your souvenir from the firm. A present. From the director himself. Upon the completion of a successful experiment."

"Great," said the young man on assignment. "But take the box out of here. We've got a job to do."

"I want you to undress."

"I am undressed. "

"But how long will you stay under that sheet?"

"But... but why?"

She holds onto the sheet anyway and even clasps it to her body.

"Leave then," he says. "I can't do it like that, you're turning me off."

Humiliated, and still holding onto the sheet, she starts to get up from the warm bed where she'd been lying with him so long. She's leaving. He gives her three or four seconds (he knows he can always get up and catch her, even at the door). But he's sure that with her limited intelligence she won't be able to endure the hurt of leaving—and he's right: sobbing, she returns to the bed and stands there. She still clasps the sheet.

Now that he's won, he's tender. He gets up slowly and stands beside her, takes away the sheet (looking in her eyes)—and then once again there's silence and the bed.

"Come over here."

She cries, "But I am here. I've been here the whole time... Why are you confusing me? I'm here with you. Don't do that. I don't understand at all..." And her breathing is upset, like her thoughts, the words she speaks fall apart into separate sounds, not quite moans, but no longer words, and then, soon, they are moans.

Crumpled sheets. Body heat. She's breathing so noisily. (Even in her inability to cope with breathing she was simple.) He was lying there with his eyes half-closed, already resting, in the momentary glow of passion. Release. He placed his hand carefully on his heart—it was all right, it was fine, it certainly didn't need to work so hard every day or night, but, come on now, don't feel sorry for your heart, enjoy yourself, don't go easy on it, let it do a little hard work... He smiled as he imagined a small internal pump of muscle fiber driving blood through the body in powerful spurts. I'm young, he thought, how lucky I am to be young and to be able to strain my heart (and to want to). How lucky! He listened to her breathing again. She still moaned quietly from time to time, holding onto what she could of the moments just ended. He liked her troubled breathing, the shudders of her body, and what seemed to be a regular refrain of soft emotional cries. Perhaps it was partly because of her job? Or because of her mental backwardness? Maybe both.

He touched her shoulder with his hand, and she instantly trembled from the contact. A feverish shudder, such as women gave only in earlier times. The way our great-great-great-great-grandmothers did it. He was amused by the thought that from the point of view of human evolution, he was now lying in bed with a woman who had been completely defined by the commonness of her own fate, like a woman from the twentieth or nineteenth century, for instance. Or even the eighteenth! She was a national treasure.

That's why, even in distant times, intellectuals were so fond of simple women, it's a well-established and probably eternal attraction...

The ringing interrupted his thought.

"Yes," he said.

The technical engineer reported that the conveyor had been set for tomorrow's link-up of the asssembly. Everything was ready...

"Tomorrow at nine sharp in the room you know so well."

"No," the man on assignment said. "I want to begin at the initial point. I was promised that. I want to take my chronometers along the line from point zero all the way to my assembly."

"But then you won't see the link-up of the ATm-241."

"I can watch it simultaneously on the screen."

"But how can you... it's your baby, the second when the line is cut in two, the moment when it's connected... Really, don't you want to watch it in person?"

"I care more about the seconds."

There was a pause. And then the technical engineer was speaking to Pops (ah, Pops was there!), saying the newcomer insisted on starting at the starting point—point zero.

Pops hemmed and hawed.

The young man on assignment became more insistent and broke into their negotiations, "Yes, I do! I'm certain about the twenty-six seconds and I don't want them lost along the way. You'll report to the management that forty seconds were lost, and as soon as I leave, you'll say that you managed on your own to confine it to twenty-six, for which you'll probably receive some stupid boxes as a prize! I know those tricks!" He was going too far, of course, and did it intentionally.

"He insists," the technical engineer told Pops for the second time.

Pops gave his consent—eight a.m. at point zero.

For a second the young man could see his assembly again: the ATm-241 was standing just as it had been assembled right before he left, it was ready to run, its silver surfaces shone. Never mind. On the screen it would look even more beautiful and silvery. Still, how amazing it is when our ideas have taken on physical form—we intuitively suppose that if we've made order out of chaos, if we've created an *assembly* in some place out of nothing, then we've improved not only nature but our very selves. (By ordering chaos into an assembly, we've also ordered the chaos in some secluded part of our soul.) This age-old illusion recurs every time, perhaps as a reward and gift, or, perhaps, it's man's eternal curse—hope, the eternal, ever-present attempt to soar without wings.

"Remember, though, that only volunteers work at the initial point of the cycle. They're our best workers, the volunteers."

"I'll remember," the young man said. He put down the receiver and turned his thoughts again to the room (where he was and where she was). "The old man's obsessed with his volunteers," he thought.

She was lying with the sheet pulled all the way to her chin, and with one hand showing—as if hoping that if he wanted to touch her, he'd touch her hand first. He saw her face. And the extended hand.

"From two centuries ago," he thought, and immediately noted that he'd just given her another century, added time, and consequently she was expanding. "Maybe she even believes in God. Unconsciously, of course..."

He pulled off the sheet to see her naked—the light of the moon was weak tonight. Olya drew up her knees, squeezed herself into a ball, covered her breasts with an arm and broke into tears.

"What is it, what's wrong?" He sat down closer to her, hugged and kissed her.

Above them on the wall was an abstraction. An abstract painting. A delicate web of lines and patches of color. RAPHAEL PURSUED THIS, TOO—an inscription to hearten all artists. It was the title of the picture. A modest title. An imitation of maturity, but not eternity. RAPHAEL PURSUED THIS, TOO popped into his eyes again as it slid down the wall. Had he improved the smell of slaughter with his own art? Or pursued love? Ah yes, he'd pursued this and that. That was the point—*both this and that.*

She was talking about her life. She lived in a dormitory. She had a small apartment there and lived by herself. She had two girlfriends and one was going to get married, yes, to a local guy, of course. He drove a bulldozer.

And she didn't just clean the guest houses, she tended the cows too. Where did all the cows here come from? Oh them, they're farmed out for the season. Probably a part of the secret enterprise's huge territory is used for pastureland—the cows, thank God, don't take information out. There's cheese and butter. All very cheap. Maybe by agreement with a dairy.

"...My cows always sense I'm taking care of them. I stroke them. I wash their udders. You might wonder what's so special about washing udders. But it's not so simple. Hoses don't work. You've got to use your hands. I feel around very gently. I clean off everything that's stuck on. Every little lump of dirt and manure that's there, every bit of straw—the straw sticks to them. And the cows understand..."

"You have beautiful hands... But don't hide now, don't hide yourself. You really are strange!"

An unmistakable signal sounded. Beep-beep-beep-beep... Wrapping herself in the sheet, she stumbled out of bed and rushed over to the small table where she'd left her little radio phone, which stood out darkly in the distance, like an oblong bar of chocolate. She turned on the receiver.

"I'm listening."

They instructed, "Tomorrow's schedule. Don't go to clean the guest houses, go to milk the cows. Repeat."

"Tomorrow I don't clean. I milk the cows."

"Correct. How do you feel?"

"Good. Thank you."

"Good night."

And instead of a disconnect signal there were a few bars of a popular song.

From the communication it was clear that he and she would not see each other the following day—that this evening was their last. So, that was it then. He said he'd have some wine. She asked if he wouldn't be too tired before tomorrow's test, wasn't she disturbing him, she'd leave right away if he said to.

"No," he said with a smile and felt the youth inside him again.

"I took to..." she said.

In his own happy and lighthearted frame of mind, he thought (he wasn't paying much attention) that Olya was talking about him, about the feelings that had been ignited between them during this short time, but now he broke into laughter, for it seemed she was talking about cows again (having a sentimental nature, she was telling him about her life), "I took to them so quickly. I have different names for them all. Like in childhood. But as soon as I've washed them a few times, they're taken away."

"They can't be kept here all the time."

"They say they're herded into a long train and taken away."

"If you like cows so much, then go work at the dairy."

"The machinery is so complicated there. I'm only able to straighten things up and wash... I was sick as a child, and my head was hurt."

"Enough about that."

He drew her closer.

Her eyes had filled with tears. Olya cried without realizing that she was crying. The tears just stayed in her eyes. "Come on," he said. "It's a good place for you, no one hurts you... Plant some sunflowers for yourself near the dormitory. Right under the windows. And every morning think about your childhood and the Ukraine."

She was delighted—what a good idea he'd given her, why hadn't she thought of planting sunflowers for herself.

"...eyes."

"Not like your two girlfriends have?" he laughed.

"Completely different. They're restless. You're smart and very restless."

He kept on grinning, "And does that bother you? My restlessness?"

"No... Yes... Mostly..."

She became confused and fell silent, as happens with people who live the same routine day after day.

A thought flashed in his mind, which was accustomed to analytical thinking and open to the emergence of the most unexpected variables. But it was just a flash and then it was gone.

Still he asked, "So you think that the cows here are taken away somewhere?"

"That's right."

"On trains?"

"Yes."

But he was already thinking about her amazing inner world again, which was deficient in learning, underdeveloped, and small, and yet preserved all the half-forgotten psychological nuances of the distant past.

"Tell me what you're feeling now."

She doesn't really answer. "I feel fine. I forgot where I... An uncomfortable house. I can't see it when I look. I think I'll remember for a long time..."

She was mumbling this way while lying beside him—the depletion of desire. He sensed that he'd probably come to feel sorry for her. That happens. An unexpected weight on the heart. It's always that way when you expose something: you want to undress it, expose it, see it in truth and nakedness, and then it becomes more precious to you, he noted.

He walked part of the way with her.

They walked past both guest houses. On the left rose the blind wall of the plant buildings, but there was an asphalt walk that curved around it and a rather dense row of streetlamps stretching along the path. It was three in the morning. A guard appeared. The men checked their documents.

The sharply curving asphalt walk led to a square from which the residential buildings were visible. In the semidarkness you could still see a small spring with a white dam, a small bridge leading across the dam, and a large willow near the bridge. They stopped here and parted. The willow was an old giant sprawling tree, and the shrubs all around it were offshoots of the mother tree.

3

They let him in through the door with the "zero" sign on it, and from the corridor he stepped straight into an ocean of air—the vast expanse of the stockyard. A cement arena with patches of meadow and real green grass, which probably was sprinkled frequently and grew fast. Farther on began an overhead conveyor with fodder and high-quality straw the color of light. Some cows were standing, some were lying down. They chewed. The cows mooed and constantly wriggled their ears. They were flexing their horns, and yet they remained majestically calm. The roundup had already begun.

The cows seemed to move forward on their own. They were directed by tiny speakers mounted in the cement, which broadcast a continuous "Git! Git! Git!" that was recorded on tape as well as a superbly recorded whistling whip—why beat if you can act on the mind. Then came the sharp half-blow, half-shot of a belt striking—a nearby cow trembled all over—and a simple "fuck it!" followed by a splendid variety of first-rate old-fashioned obscenities. And the cows moved by themselves in the direction of the cement chutes. Yes, by themselves. He saw it clearly.

The older cows were the first to run in, those who had lived a lifetime and were for that reason the most ready and obedient. Shaking their worn, emptied udders, they clomped ahead loudly and unashamedly, with lowered heads and horns. They limped along on noticeably tired legs, but even those who were shoved in the dark and even those who stumbled were obedient and ready and tried to show that their lameness and pain were nothing at all—a small matter—and they would overcome it, let it be clear, despite their pain, that they were the first ones ready and they had made peace with their end. They neither expected, nor did they ever dream, that somewhere a special train was waiting for them and they would be taken far away to a place where grass would grow to their bellies and sunflowers sway over the grass and the sun would slide slowly down into the night.

The man on assignment crossed over a light suspension bridge (made expressly for observation) to the side where the cows were running, heading toward a narrow opening in the chute. A man could stand off to the side and above them at the same time. As it was given to men to do.

Swept along by the flow and the common readiness, the younger cows also began to run. Separate herds intermingled. A small group of black cows with tiny white stars on their foreheads refused to break up for any reason, and as a result at the turn to the cement chute there was, well, no, not a standstill, but somewhat of a delay. The black cows stood firm, even digging in their heels, stretched out their horns, and tried to keep chewing the grass. But the common stream flowed on around them, shoving one after another off to the side and tearing away the ones at the edge, carrying them along until they all—the black cows with the tiny white stars on their foreheads—were completely intermingled and taken up into the stream.

Unwittingly the man on assignment noticed a black and white cow below, running almost directly beneath him; she was very dark, but with white splashes—blazes of white. Her bearing was striking, she gave no sign of fatigue. The speed was drawing all of them in; naturally, she was caught up too. And he lost her. She was no longer there. Her hoofs were clattering somewhere in that scattered thousandfold rumbling and drumming of hoofs. Just then the small chronometer that hung over the shoulder of the man on assignment began to blink. Oh! The screen lit up. It was small, about the size of a palm, but the definition was great. There was a clear picture of the heads of the technical engineer and Pops as they bent over their work—the link-up had begun. The young man on assignment noted the time—he wouldn't give them his seconds.

The broad-muzzled, rosy, and sleek calves had also stubbornly dug in their heels in one spot, so the whistle of the whip and the recorded "damn fuckers" boomed out again, this time at an almost deafening volume; moreover, one of two drovers (they were paired up; the man on assignment saw the volunteers with his own eyes now) jumped inside the fence and fearlessly chased out the sluggish calves, poking them under the ribs with an empty milk bottle, which he'd apparently just finished drinking.

The herd entered—the man on assignment walked along behind them above one of the chutes that the cows were running into in groups of four or five across. Now he found himself looking down on a large cement hall.

The concealed pores in the cement floor had been opened slightly, there were minute holes from which very fine jets of water shot out. Seen from a distance, the jets seemed like little drinking fountains, but then the water started to shoot with greater force in order to wash the cattle and to remove the dust of the road from their bodies. Clumps of hardened dung and straw floated on the floor. The cows took the water as a good sign. They stretched out their muzzles, trying to catch the pulsating streams and take one more long drink, but even if they didn't get a drink it felt good to them anyway—it was water, and ablution is always something sacred. Their eyes began to shine. Their moist horns began to shine, and the clefts of their hoofs stood out clearly. But then the streams turned fine again, becoming almost weightless; they brushed over the cows' flanks and bounced off, only to spurt higher and form sparkling fountains over the cows' heads on which danced dozens of rainbows, created from the reflected, scattered light. Now the women entered through the door to the compound. Wearing scarves on their heads and overalls, they moved gently among the cows. When cows become anxious, they secrete harmful and toxic substances that race through their bodies, and that's why these simple nice young women stand near them—the simplest and most unreflective women are selected to work here, and it's best if they are even a little backward in their development. The women were good-natured and made easy contact with the animals, walking back and forth through the rows of cows and doing a kind of supplementary, final wash; they looked at the udders, for instance, checking whether anything had stuck to the soft tissue, they ran their hands over the flanks and stroked them—as they did this, they walked rather quickly, just barely touching the cows' bodies and addressing each cow by a general name, "C'mere, Zorka, dear. Let me have your udder... Let me have it, don't kick, come on, Burenka." The quiet voices calmed them and the cows trusted again. Suddenly they began to extend their muzzles and nudge the human arms and hands, and their bellowing became more of a sweet and very soft moo. The young women smiled, sensing the cow soul without any effort. "There, there, sweet. It's all right. Everything's all right," they said as they passed. A rite. Dozens of kind cow faces turned to follow—thus it was at the very beginning of their docile domestication thousands of years ago. And after the young women walked by, the fountains disappeared too, though microscopic bubbles of moisture remained in the air—yellow, blue, bright orange—and the dance of rainbows.

In the midst of the driven herd suddenly he once again spotted the stately black cow with the blazes of light on her sides. A particular instance of fate. Without being very conscious of it, he had intermittently looked for her. His memory was stirred. Compassion is always relative. "In order to determine other speeds, one must assume a certain speed as a constant," he remembered.

At the same time, naturally, the young man on assignment watched his small screen—the technical engineer and two of his assistants were quickly and adroitly connecting the drives and the dozens of small tubes and hoses of his ATm-241 assembly. Pops stood right next to them, never taking his eyes off the chronometer—about half an hour remained, no longer. The man on assignment made a note—half an hour...

A narrow passage opened in the cement chute, and the clean cows went through by themselves, the slant of the floor easing their way. As many as could get in filled the cement rooms—*box stalls*—he remembered the term. The computers that extrapolated the cows' nutritional condition probably checked their actual live weight. The data was transmitted to a relay board so that at a given moment (when the weight limit was reached) a partition made of iron grating was released—it slid down quietly, without any noise; that's right, don't alarm them, everything operates with positive emotions—Raphael pursued this too. It slid down slowly, and separated these from those. And they (these) were swallowed by the dark.

To see them again one had to look for an entrance that was lit; there had to be an entrance, of course, and the young man on assignment looked around until he saw the small door. "Boxes," he repeated, with certainty now. "Two centuries ago... Well, how can you modernize what has to be kept secret all the time."

* * *

The cows were relatively calm and free while standing in the boxes. They'd gone in willingly, after all, they hadn't been driven in. They swung their muzzles back and forth and lowered their wet horns. Some of them would suddenly moo, a friendly reminder that feeding time was near. As they were being washed by the jets of water, they'd managed to quench some of their thirst with water from the floor. Well, what of it, sometimes people are late with the feeding–then you have to moo. Some of them scratched themselves against the chrome-plated–God save us from rust–walls of the boxes.

From the upper bridge the man on assignment could see several boxes right away, the angle of vision allowed him to take in five or six of the cement pens. A few men stood near the boxes in small atrium-niches–they were the workers who stunned the animals, it was all just as it had been some two hundred years ago (needless to say, volunteers are needed for places that haven't been modernized yet, but it was also possible that people got big money for doing the stunning).

The red arrow on the display board approached the mark PLANKS; one of the volunteers was already on his way there. He wasn't supposed to hurry. But despite the slow flow of time, despite the fact that he'd taken only a few steps in the direction of the knife switch, a biopsychic wave engulfed the animals. They raised their heads, stretched out their necks, and stiffened with fright as they looked up somewhere, maybe toward a heaven not visible from here, a place from which, so they might reflect, their life had come and they'd been given the green grass in the meadows, a calf at the udder, and the moon at night. They didn't know whom to appeal to, neither a name, nor even a word that might bring them close. The young man on assignment looked carefully: their long white eyelashes didn't blink any more often than usual, their eyes hadn't filled up–there was just a touch of moisture around the eyelids, no more than during an ordinary request. As the man was taking his short (but calm) steps toward the switch, a final understanding came into their unblinking eyes, but this final understanding was also perfectly humble.

"Listen," said the young man on assignment, speaking into his chronometer set with the screen and the radio. "Listen. We stopped killing animals ages ago."

"That's what you think," Pops's voice grumbled over the radio.

"That's what the majority of people think. The vast majority."

"Let them go on thinking it."

"There must be something else to feed people with."

"There isn't. We've always killed and we'll keep on killing. Synthetic protein exists, of course. But, all things considered, the main protein's right here."

"But do other countries do the same?"

"Of course. The whole world runs the same way. All of us have killed and we'll all continue to kill. Excuse me, I'm busy..."

Pops bent over the transducers that monitored the movement (the crawl) of the test mash, which wouldn't be used in the product and was intended only to clean out the inner surfaces of the ATm-241. The man on assignment now remembered, and in detail, how the very same secretiveness had prevailed when he was on trips abroad; the very same evasive, often ambiguous, answers came from the specialists—all those who had known the synthesizing process from the start.

"Listen," he said one more time. But he couldn't stop himself from taking his eyes off the screen, and now he was staring intently at the boxes. Wham! The jolt of current was so strong that the cows shot up—they flew into the air. And their large eyes shot up and out with an even greater force, the eyes burst as if the cows had been hit on top of the head with a hammer that could smash cement. The cows were thrown almost a meter high from the planks, and the spasms started to shoot through their bodies when they were still on the way down. Their legs and rumps and heads and horns were twitching as though the cows were insects with brittle and delicate extremities.

Finally the spasms weakened, and the bodies of the cows crowded the floor. Their despairing souls had been taken to our common eternity, and what remained was only a play of nerve fibers, which twitched and throbbed by themselves now; just in case, the volunteers poked the cows with their electric goads again, and the cows' mouths opened wide and fell apart, the metal points of the goads poked into the enormous drooping tongues, and streams of yellow sparks poured forth. The volunteers managed to jump aside, the floor of the boxes was dropped, and the cows slid down along those same chrome-covered planks into pits, as into the nether world. Where there was an end and also a beginning. One could see that chains had been thrown around the cows' legs, the carcasses were hoisted, and thus bound in chains, their heads and horns facing the ground, the cows embarked upon their final journey. They seemed to move slowly with heads down and legs up, as if they were mere reflections moving along a clear pond at watering time. Suspended, they swung back and forth, which intensified the appearance of motion. One after another, swinging, bumping a little at times, just like at the watering hole, the reflected herd passed through the gates of the plant buildings. The hooked chains they hung from were swinging less loudly now. The herd passed on. They moved toward the large troughs. And they truly wanted to drink—their dead mouths hung open and the large tongues drooped from their own weight, but instead of the saliva that usually forms right before mastication only spumous bloody pus trickled out. The last to pass were the upside-down stubborn calves.

"The ATm-241 is connected to the main conveyor," Pops's voice reported.

But the technical engineer (on screen), who knew that the man on assignment was watching them intently now, gestured, as if to say: Everything's fine!

The man on assignment marked the second of connection on his control chronometer. But it was clear that he was staying quiet for a long time. It was clear that he wasn't responding emotionally or saying anything at all to mark the moment when his assembly was connected. After a click Pops's voice came on, "Just don't start imagining, please, that you're an accomplice," he said brusquely. "In that case we're all accomplices. All those who make the metal panels and the instruments, and those who mine the ore the metal is smelted from, and those who feed those who mine the ore..."

The young man on assignment was annoyed that they were trying to comfort him, and he shouted, "All right, I get it! Business as usual."

On the screen he saw his assembly already at work, filtering toxic substances from the meat of cows that probably had been killed several hours earlier (the conveyor works at night, too). The smell of blood, which he knew so well now, stabbed his nostrils. The smell of blood–and immediately the natural thought appeared: maybe he had seen the grass and the clouds in the sky today for the last time? He knew too much now, and they lived here, after all, *like men from the last century.* He immediately qualified this: *like men from the century before last, and from all the previous centuries.* He remembered how he'd fought for point zero and the technical engineer had lowered his voice and told Pops, "He insists..."

The fear receded. (Something inside him shook, then steadied.) They weren't likely to kill him, of course, but wouldn't they shut him up here forever? They could tell his office that he'd gone mad. Or that he'd become one of the volunteers. You could expect anything from them.

Oh, yes, now he knew what that smell had been–and why the wave of instinctive fear had overcome him.

The shackled carcasses (of the reflected, upside-down cows) moved toward a trough where a man who was wearing an apron over protective leather coveralls stood, bending the cows' muzzles a little farther over the trough. He was watering them–no, one can't say that–he was watering them antipodally, watering in reverse: skillfully puncturing their veins. When the neck is drawn down by the weight of the head it's easy to puncture the veins—a stream gushed out immediately with great force and no sooner had blood filled the empty trough than another cow came "to drink"; another vein and another red stream shot into the trough. The air conditioners droned on, but the thick red smell hung there and eclipsed everything—it was stifling.

His signature on the secrecy agreement? So what? I didn't see or hear a thing, he thought, and he saw and heard how the ears of the cows were chopped off with sharp butcher knives along both sides of the conveyor (a pile of cows' ears had risen on his side of the bridge). The next man on the conveyor line was using a scalpel to cut the skin along the forehead loose in a special way so that the next man down the line, by thrusting his hand beneath the skin on the cow's head, could twist the neck vertebrae and then with one quick, though difficult, professional tug, pull the cow's head out of its skin, so that it came out naked, but with eyes. Because of the network of capillaries protruding everywhere, the naked white head instantly turned red, and no sooner was it colored than they hung it—by itself and rather solemnly—on a hook, and then it sailed off to the side, branching onto a separate narrow conveyor just for heads. One head after another. In single file and rather solemnly. The crazed gaze of the eyes gave one to know that even though a terrible price had been paid, the heads had recovered the downward gaze that nature had provided them, a true gaze, not reversed, as in a reflection. But that true gaze was also their last: their eyes were scraped out with an extra-sharp scoop and tossed aside to the left and right. A pile of ears. A pile of eyes. I didn't see or hear a thing... And the heads on the hooks sailed on to the next processing station, from which the mosquito-like screech of a saw could be heard and where horns were being sawed off and were rising in their own pile, which resembled the pile of goblets that soldiers of Svyatoslav's time hurled down after one of their feasts.*

*Svyatoslav Igorovich, Grand Prince of Kiev in the tenth century and a celebrated warrior [*tr.*].

The carcasses were pulled across a lathe and split open. The workers tore out the connective tissue under the skin and cut through the tendons. There was a crack and a crunch—they turned the skin inside out and pulled it off, leaving each carcass completely white, bare, and defenseless, surrounded only by the light steam that rose from it, its sole covering at this ashamed moment of departure which evoked the body's first moment in the world—the moment of birth.

The man on assignment transferred his eyes to the empty screen where an image was now forming—the outline of his assembly, his ATm-241, appeared against a flickering background—it had been linked to the central computer and was already up and running. "Did you take the section 11 bridge back?" Pops's voice asked.

"I didn't notice the number but I came the right way. I'm following the pieces of meat that are crawling toward my assembly on the narrow-track conveyor."

"Right."

He still had two or three minutes to go. Another turn. And there was his room (a small plaque had already been placed there for all time: ATm-241).

"You're doing good work," Pops said.

"I'm trying my best."

And the technical engineer shook his hand. The three of them were in the room. The workers had left. The assembly was in full swing. Pops and the technical engineer were looking at their chronometers and the man on assignment at his, and they'd keep on looking until the chunks of meat and the sausage that inched along the narrow-track conveyor reached the ATm-241 and passed through, after which all three would check the time—their time and his.

"You can stay on at the plant for a few more days. Look over everything more carefully. Do some analyses," Pops said, and there was a note of pleading in his voice.

They would let him go for now.

"Everything's going smoothly," the technical engineer declared.

***

It got dark fast. The south. In his guest house the man on assignment sat at the desk with the analyzer in front of him and carefully entered all of the data into the central computer, but his thoughts were not about work now—he was thinking about himself, how he'd gotten himself into danger so quickly. That's what people get for being curious. Would he have to live here forever... with no way out? (Condemned for having discovered evil?)

He turned off the light and lay down, but then got up and walked to the window. The moon was out. That was good. Dressed only in his light summer trousers and a light shirt, with no provisions at all on him (no one would think he was trying to escape), he climbed out the open window. His feet landed on soft grass. He kept on walking over the grass, and in the moonlight he could see a few scattered trees. After half an hour of brisk and cautious walking he came to the outer wall. Here the wall ran in a straight line to the left and to the right it turned, making a slight curve. He went closer—it was old brickwork, not more than two and a half meters high. He took a leap and without any trouble grabbed onto the edge.

No one could escape across the steppe—they'd die on the way—but his idea was this: he would walk a bit further into the steppe and make a bonfire to attract one of the helicopters that flew over on regularly scheduled flights. From the air a fire can be seen from far away. If there was no flight that night, he'd return to the plant and continue to work hunched over the computer in his guest house. He'd let the fire burn for an hour, maybe two—that would be enough, there was a chance. Of course, it was also dangerous.

The moon helped him to see the groove running along the top of the wall. He leapt up, grabbed on to the edge and pulled himself up. He made it. He squatted on top of the brick wall (the wall turned out to be almost a meter wide) and looked into the distance. The moon. And the steppe. Pale white streaks flowed out toward the horizon—

was it the steppe grass glowing in the moonlight? Or had the wind spread strips across the steppe?... What an enormous, vast space lies ahead–and all ours! he quipped to himself, "ours" meaning that *we* have to cross it. He knew enough for today; it was time to go back.

He heard the rustle of wings. A steppe bird flew overhead. Somewhere in the brick groove she had her nest.

The next day he worked hard; he was trying his best. They were killers, they were killing animals, but the assembly was his. (His idea and his work.) And, besides, the more earnestly he worked, the less noticeable his preparations for escape would be.

The more thoroughly he did his work, the greater his moral right to leave. He'd finish his work. And that would be it. The doors of the boxes had been washed white. Limed innocence. Some of the fallen calves had still moved a little when the volunteers walked by with their electric goads. The men would touch the calves' lips, or tongues, if the tongues hung out, with the copper (sometimes silver) tip of the goads. They touched very lightly and carefully, here and there, without stabbing or slashing, with no spurts of blood–not at all like a bullfight. A light touch, the calf shuddered a little–and that was all...

We'll leave our hero here. He knows almost everything about life now–he's discovered the evil in the world.

The hero and his (quite ordinary) story were born, one could say, from conversation. Conversation with my friend Ilya Ivanovich, an ordinary engineer who worked in an ordinary scientific research institute.

Ilya Ivanovich couldn't bear the pain of any person, animal, or bird. It's unpleasant for any of us to see such suffering and so at the moment it occurs we just close our eyes (literally or figuratively), but Ilya Ivanovich wasn't able to close his eyes, and as a result the poor man found life and its experiences more than he could take.

That's how I started talking with him about the animals that are killed for meat and the round-up of homeless dogs and cats—about the evil we commit every day.

In a certain sense, an enormous killing field is created around every slaughterhouse or horse-flayer's yard, and that field unquestionably affects people—it penetrates their consciousness and influences their instincts.

But how can we fight it—how? The problem seems insoluble.

I frequently talked about all these things with Ilya; that's what I still call him sometimes from force of habit. (Old memories are strong, I remember very well how Ilya and I lived in the same room when we were students, there was a third person as well. I remember that one day—I can't say why—we suffered a fit of laughter, laughing boisterously with all the energy of youth and Ilya even collapsed onto the bed and lay there on his back dangling his legs. We were doubled over with laughter and Ilya was kicking his legs and snorting. It was as if he were running through the air.)

After we grew up and went our separate ways, Ilya Ivanovich and I kept up a friendship of sorts—though a rather distant one. We weren't able to see each other for years; we lived our separate lives.

And it was only quite recently, shortly before he died, that I learned he'd become abnormally sensitive to the pain of others.

In that respect—his abnormal sensitivity to pain—he was a most unusual person, unique even, and if his death passed largely unnoticed by people, it's not surprising. But the fact that nature (which is itself so sensitive and vulnerable) didn't notice his death, didn't mark it with some sign or revelation—that's what's unjust, in my view. People didn't notice, but neither did nature mark it with anything, except a moonlit night. On that moonlit night he died.

***

We often talked about the time when there would be no more wars or civil unrest and when people would no longer kill other people—even in daily life with a household knife or flat iron; and when criminal life would also have ceased. No longer time, but paradise.

But how would people who lived in this humane time be able to reconcile their conscience with (or conceal from it) the fact that they, human beings, still killed animals for their meat and fat and skin?

That was one of his favorite topics.

Usually I talked with Ilya Ivanovich while I was helping him get to the hospital—Ilya himself or (sometimes) his wife would ask me to do this simple favor, and I accompanied him. And you have to have something to talk about with the person you're taking to the hospital.

4

Even today, to a certain degree, people conceal things; for instance, they'll avoid mentioning, say, the extermination of homeless dogs—newspapers are full of all sorts of stories, but have no reports about the animals we kill. Who do we conceal this from? Ourselves, of course. There exists a sacred agreement, as it were—to behave and live in such a way that people will remember less and less about the animals that are simply murdered, especially the ones killed for meat.

The fact is that otherwise people become hardened, especially the young.

Why don't we condone the slaughter of dogs on the street, after all, or even the slaying of just one dog when a hunter has to try out his rifle? Why do we tell our children in such touching words that dogs should be loved—is it for the dogs? Not in the least. We do this, like everything we do, for ourselves. For our own sake, so as not to foster more cruelty in ourselves (especially in our children and youth), inasmuch as there is plenty around already, and at any moment more can come back to us, even from the animals we kill.

According to the statistics, eighty-five thousand dogs were exterminated in one year in Leningrad alone, and not to make soap, either. Soap is not meat; piles of soap can be produced by chemical means. But how can we feed the ever growing number of dogs being born? And how can sanitary conditions be maintained? In any case, in just that one large city on the Neva eighty-five thousand dogs were killed in one year and over a hundred thousand cats. Well-meaning (and not at all predatory) pitilessness. And, by the way, people are now trying to talk less about these sweeping annual actions.

Ilya Ivanovich and I would discuss how this could be fixed. Naturally, it takes effort and hard work. Regulation of the cat population, selection, control of mating—and before you know it we'll have only as many beloved house pets as we need. As is the situation with parrots, for example. Or marmosets, which also live in the city, after all, and which people, out of love, also keep in apartments, hundreds of them, but don't allow to propagate to the extent that there are monkeys jumping around on our heads in the subway, tearing off hats and messing up women's makeup.

The next matter, we agreed, is more complicated. What can be done about those animals we call cows? Or sheep?

After all, we do eat them. Even though we try not to think about it and not to remember. The more our humanism and morality develop, the more convincingly we'll have to speak (at least to children) about our good relations with animals—and the more we must close our eyes to the fact that we kill them and eat their meat.

Even now we kill animals in considerable secrecy, the secrecy of silence, and we push this secret into our deepest depths (but territorially—far in the distance, behind the fence, somewhere on the outskirts of the city).

There won't be any political prisoners in the camps either, of course. Dissidents will be looked upon as prophets: sometimes they make mistakes, but at other times, they light up the road for us like the beam of a searchlight (sometimes their life will be difficult, sometimes triumphant). In any event, it's clear that people won't be herded into camps in great numbers, nor will individuals be jailed on political charges. Even ordinary crime will end. The final throes of statistics (five murders, four, three, two... one)—and then no more murder and no more roundups—golden days will come, and not only because of legal prohibitions and humanism. One day it will seem as savage and absurd to kill a human as to eat human flesh.

Humanism's great strength, as we know, lies in its ability to nourish the soul and all aspects of our daily life. Even today we protect animals, forbidding people to beat dogs on the street or mistreat cats or pigeons, and all so as not to upset the balance of good and evil in ourselves, where, we'd like to think, the tray of good on the scales is still a little bit heavier. Thousands of novels and countless movies on TV will be used to shape public opinion. The mistreatment of a dog will be tried in public in every country. The criminal law code will contain many articles—Article 132 section C, Article 156 section B and so on, with appropriately severe penalties. Legalistic, but not boring. A child knows from early on that killing a dog is bad, but he doesn't know that killing a million cows isn't bad. Whose eyes are sadder, the dog's or the cow's? A very simple honest question.

And one way or another the matter must be hushed up or hidden not only from the child, but from the educated intelligent adult as well; certainly, the plain facts about murder can't be dangled before his eyes, "I think," you tell him evasively, "they're still being killed somewhere. Though apparently not here. Somewhere far away. Somewhere... someone..." The refinement of mind and psyche as well as the general expansion of humanism into art and then into everyday life will make the concept of killing animals intolerable. The simple realization of its total injustice (killing animals at a time when people have long ago stopped killing each other) might even cause a sensitive and easily upset intellectual to commit suicide after he's discovered the scandalous and secretly sanctioned slaughter of animals—after all, he has also eaten meat and, therefore, he has sanctioned it too.

He'll commit suicide—but this means he will have been killed (and, consequently, won't we be killing people again?).

Even one suicide of this kind, then, will suffice to discourage discussion about the slaughter of animals. People will hide the secret of meat. Of course, we'll just be feeling sorry for ourselves again, protecting ourselves, just as we always do in every matter (how we protest our love for lakes and beautiful rivers and the clear sky, and it's ourselves we feel sorry for and not the lakes and the clear heavenly air, we want to protect ourselves, that's what it's all about!). And for precisely this reason the time will come when the killing of animals will be a forbidden topic from childhood on; from the first steps we take till the time we're gray, we'll be kept in the dark about where it comes from, this tender or even slightly tough meat, which we so happily eat. Even today we conceal the facts from children. Next it will be teenagers. But the wave of suicides of vulnerable young people—our children!—will convince us that the best road to take will be (on the one hand) to develop the production of artificial protein and (on the other) to keep the existing slaughterhouses a secret. Gradually, of course, gradually. First we must lower the numbers, and then with the help of the mass media we must lie about, and inflate, the amount of artificial synthetic protein in use, the successes of advanced technology, the millions of tons of meat (indistinguishable from real meat), and the refrigerators filled from top to bottom. Eventually–just as with the prison camps–the circle of those who know and lie about things will gradually narrow in size, be shrouded in secrecy, and (most important!) become restricted to special territories enclosed by walls. They, the ones who know, will to an increasing extent stop having *any* contact with other people. In this way the process will inevitably come to the point where *no one will know.* Although, naturally, for a certain period of time rumors will circulate and innuendos will be heard–even jokes. But gradually this talk, too, will fade. Another two or three generations and... silence. It will no longer be mentioned; nothing of the sort exists, they'll say. Not any more. And people will have accepted it already–nothing of that sort exists any more.

The slaughterhouses (regardless of whether they are old-fashioned or equipped with modern technology) will be moved farther and farther away to places deep within the steppe. And the process itself, as well as the people taking part in it, and the conveyors, and the cattle taken there in closed cars, will be plunged into secrecy and cover-up, like everything that is denied.

Such were the discussions Ilya Ivanovich and I had on our way to the clinic. The hospital complex with its surrounding brick wall loomed closer with each step we took. Just as the brick wall of the plant and testing ground with its arched "WELCOME" sign had loomed up out of the feather-grass and wormwood steppe before the young man (the one from the future, who'd so cleverly invented the ATm-241).

This isn't an analogy, just a visual correspondence in external appearance–coincidence.

People everywhere will believe that cows are only milked, that they generously give us milk and cheese, and when the cows get old they're let out to pasture, where they die a natural death. They're like people. Almost like people, only somewhere far away in the steppe. And thousands of scientific research institutes will be hard at work so that off in the distant slaughterhouses they'll get better and better at removing the smell of living adrenaline from meat and its blood, for people's morality will continue to evolve, and that being so, they'll be that much more sensitive to the smell of murder. And some day we'll reach such a height of universal morality that it will be simply unthinkable for people to speak openly about what man is really made of.

They'll no longer be able to hear or read about slaughterhouses, it will pain them, cut to the heart, they'll feel sick, they might die, they'll break down psychologically.

And then will come the moment when the fact that we kill animals for food has to be covered up, just as in our time we cover up the military's missile units or the last secret prison camp for dissidents. What can one do—the two things are incompatible. The ordinary slaughterhouse, which today is part of every city's meat industry, becomes a secret... A golden age! People don't go to war. People are certain that they eat meat made only from synthetic and partly vegetable protein—meat made from grain, or meat made from seaweed.

The newspapers are full of the discoveries of the newest meat substitutes (one discovery overtakes another). It's discussed in government circles as well as simply on the street, just as today we discuss the success of the Japanese in electronics and the success of the Americans with their many flights in space.

Every evening the TV news program shows whole reservoirs full of artificial protein, various strains out of which talented experts, utilizing the latest technology, make, or to put it better, create, pieces of genuine meat right before the eyes of the television viewers. (What fantastic hygiene! And a design by Miro!)

Yes, small pieces of meat. As if they were freshly cut. You can't tell the difference at all.

And this is when the young man who invented the ATm-241 surfaced on his own—he entered life, happy, young, and full of energy, and on his very first work assignment, he was more curious than others usually are (he insisted on following the production of protein from point zero—whatever you do, don't ever get interested in a point zero; start with the first one, for which the proud and erect figure 1 has been given us); he became curious and discovered with his own eyes that it was a killing place. Even more: not only did they kill here but also in another place and in a third place—people had never stopped killing and it was all a matter of keeping things secret.

He was shaken, of course. And yet he didn't commit suicide—that would have been too easy. He returned to his guest house—his dacha, as he jokingly called it, and continued to work. The analyzer and the computer that had been put in the guest house for him operated beautifully. The young man on assignment had three display screens on which he could trace every minute of his walk along the conveyor. (Including his moments of curiosity. There he is by the boxes. And at the disassembly point. Oh, why did he have to butt in and find out what was going on. He could have just lived his life.) But that's the way it is—we carry our baggage with us.

Patches of meadow bathed in the sun. That's where he'd started: the last green patches in the enormous concrete stockyard where the Burenkas and Zorkas nibbled on their last grass (already nibbled on by other cows, it's short, yet real grass nevertheless; while watching it again on the screen the man on assignment notices that the grass scattered before them had been mowed, it lies in clumps). Then the last ray of sun before the electric lights inside illuminate everything.

"Time—zero," the young man on assignment tells himself. He had made a mark on the video index and simultaneously picked up the stopwatch that he'd put in front of him on the table and set it at zero.

Now he needs to establish an end mark. From start to finish—that's what matters. And after that he'll replay the tape again and again, collecting the seconds and half-seconds lost on the conveyor line (but excluding those lost during the installation of his assembly).

"Here?" the man on assignment thinks (on the screen men are furiously stunning cows. They finish them off.) No, it's still too early.

He fast forwards. Aha. A moving column of cars. One car out in front, the rest being pulled behind.

This little train of cars is forging ahead, steered by a man in overalls who sits enthroned in the first car. Let's see what it carries. The small, easily handled little train is filled with spotted and white skins, which are coated with steam and still damp. The skin is like a flat sketch of a cow, rendering every feature, even, for instance, the individual markings on the leg. The final stage of violence. But if we switch to the conveyor that runs parallel to this, we'll probably see the meat already being processed... He switches—there it is. The mash is pulsing through the transparent conduit. And now we're already past Section 11. That's it. Let's fix it here. What comes later isn't of interest.

The exhausted (from the strain on his eyes) man on assignment sipped his cherry juice with ice and then called Pops—yes, he'd take into account the seconds lost by his assembly, but he'd also count the ones lost on the conveyor line.

"That's wonderful! We can only be grateful to you!" Pops shouted. "Who else would take an interest in measuring our losses."

And he asked the young man on assignment if the sound track worked. Yes, it did.

"Maybe there's something you need tonight? Something to drink? Or do you want to take a walk?"

"No, thanks. I'm going to rest."

The young man on assignment praised their analyzer. He tried not to let anything show. No superfluous remark. He shouldn't give them the opportunity to latch onto something and declare him mad or disturbed. He'd be direct, but cautious. And as soon as he finished the analysis, he'd write up his report—here, he'd say, our work's done. And then?...

He ordered a nice piece of meat for his dinner. And immediately had second thoughts—didn't that seem like a provocation?... No, let them bring it.

He went out on the porch. It got dark fast on the steppe. He walked close to the house and looked at the small garden and the vast space all around. He wouldn't let himself be tempted ahead of time. He'd breathe in the steppe, walk around the guest house once, and not take even one step from this place.

A young woman came—it was Olya. She was happy to see him, but concealed it right away—she was confused.

"You didn't leave?"

"I had to finish analyzing the material. I'll be here another two days, maybe even longer. As long as it takes."

She stood there confused. They'd said goodbye, after all. She didn't know how to behave. Would it be presumptuous or pushy if she extended her hand again...

"There, now," he said affectionately—he understood her confusion. He relieved the tension by going to her and giving her a kiss. It meant we have two more days and maybe longer to be together.

She lit up with joy, swallowing the lump in her throat. She was constantly restraining her joy because she feared it, and now it disturbed them both during love—the young woman was inhibited. He undressed her somewhat nervously while she either smiled or restrained a smile.

An hour later she said, "I have to go. There are different lectures to attend at night. We often skip them but today they warned us there will be a test."

"But don't they know you're with me?"

He didn't trust her. He asked directly (but he *might* have been thinking about the housekeeping).

"How? How would they know?" she grew flustered. She quickly dressed and left.

He sat and thought for a while. No, he didn't trust her. But, on the other hand, she was certainly naive and simple, and even if some wakeful eye watched over her—so what!

What could they gain from their relationship? Just a romance, an affair. Nothing extraordinary.

He called and asked if they'd bring him a tape of classical music. His thoughts needed inspiration. And wine, yes, he'd like more wine.

A car drove up right away, but the order was delivered by a grouchy old woman.

The analysis dragged on, every analysis goes on forever. It was the seventh day already, and the man on assignment was working conscientiously, not giving them the slightest excuse to accuse him of anything. He didn't leave the guest house. He kept his relations with the young woman extremely simple—now it was bed and pleasant conversation, no more than an hour, and then he'd walk her back.

Naturally he thought about escaping. If he filled up light plastic bottles with water and packed them in a backpack, he could venture out into the steppe. But how many kilometers did it go on for? Where would he go?... Actually, he'd heard from a snatch of conversation that people who got lost in the steppe have a real chance here: helicopters fly over—and if you can just manage to make a bonfire, the pilot will pick you up. At night if a helicopter pilot is flying his bee-shaped machine on its route and sees a bonfire—well, it's obvious that someone's gotten lost, strayed from the path, and needs to be picked up. Maybe they're even told to pick up people who appear lost? That would be a great salvation.

In order to reach the areas the helicopter passes over on its run, one has to go quite far, however. Helicopters certainly don't fly over the territory of the plant and proving ground. But that snatch of conversation about helicopter pilots picking up lost people could be a trap. They're just waiting till they can accuse him of running away and acting crazy—"He ran off into the barren steppe! What a thing to do! Does a normal man run off alone into the steppe?..."

***

In order to make a more precise calculation of the lost seconds, he played the tape on the screen while rewinding it—from the end of the film to the start. Chronometry in reverse order is more reliable: that way whoever counts the seconds is freed from what's being shown—he's less controlled by events, less likely to react empathetically. Life in reverse. The meat gradually was transformed into cows and the cows grazed on the grass. And the calculation proceeded: the seconds don't care in which direction they're counted.

He broke down the whole process into microsteps. The side conveyor appeared in a window on the left of the screen. Time was ticking away—a kasha-like mass of chopped liver began to move backwards along the conveyor, tossing out the preservatives (in the form of powder taking off), after which its color became brighter and redder, more natural, one might say. In this more wholesome state, the mash began to worm its way backward, letting itself be drawn in thin streams into the electric meat grinder (the exit place), and then after winding its way backward, it jumped out (through the entrance) as whole pieces of liver, which grew bolder and quickly slipped through a rhythmically chopping blade until once past the blade it immediately coalesced, cohering tightly and forming the enormous, brown, steam-coated liver of Zorka.

"We haven't lost a second yet!"—the voice of Pops. The sound track, obviously, was playing in forward, rather than reverse.

The young woman didn't come to his house in the evening, as usual, but ran in, all out of breath, in the middle of the day while he was working. "What's wrong?" He switched off the screen to save energy.

"I... I just thought... I talked to..."

Olya faltered.

He came closer and touched her. "What is it? Why are you so upset?"

Getting her words confused, the poor young woman answered that if he would stay on here for a while longer they could get married. She'd spoken to her friends and they all (every last one!) told her that it would be good, that if you get married, you're already a family.

"But I'm leaving soon."

"But that doesn't matter. Then I'll stay here by myself, separated. But at least I'll have been married..."

Her eyes shone with joy.

"No," he said.

"Oh, please. I beg you," her eyes dimmed.

But he had to be on his guard now.

"No," he said.

She left. After a while, after an hour or so, she contacted him on her radio phone and told him please not to be mad at her. Please forgive her. She very quietly repeated several times that everything had happened unexpectedly. Something just came over her, please forgive her.

"I'm not angry at all," he answered.

While the second hand was making its circles, he sat at the computer and entered the first data he'd collected into a long vertical column on the screen.

He phoned Pops. He let him know that he'd discovered two and a half more seconds that had been lost on the conveyor. But that wasn't all. Almost fifteen seconds had been lost at junctions.

"Excellent," Pops praised him.

"I entered everything into the central computer."

"I'll calculate everything right away. My program is linked up."

Pops's voice dropped its business-like tone, "Listen, you're an excellent worker. Why don't you get a little rest?... Come visit us. We enjoy company, we're not lone wolves, you know. We oldtimers here know how to have a good time among ourselves."

"Thanks. I'm not in the mood."

He didn't want to be with people. He wanted to be only with her.

"After I leave," he said into the phone after finding the frequency of her radio, "after I leave, you'll plant sunflowers and they'll remind you of me."

"Why?"

He had to explain, "In the morning you'll look out the window, you'll see the sunflowers and remember the person who told you to plant them..."

"O-oh!" she began to laugh quietly and gratefully.

Because the night was moonless he ran into a guard while he was out walking (he walked to the wall of the compound and back). They passed by him so calmly it seemed they hadn't noticed him. And he was only two steps away! They'd seen him but had walked on.

People from the plant (including himself) could, of course, take walks at night too, it wasn't forbidden, but right next to the wall, what carelessness! he thought. Or were they so convinced of the steppe's vastness and boundlessness that they thought no one would try to escape? It wasn't clear.

But, actually, what kind of a guard did they have here? Two or three people walking around and asking your name. Was that it?...

After reflecting on all this, the young man on assignment reached a conclusion that had been suggesting itself these last days: the conclusion that no one was keeping him here and that he had no real intention of leaving.

He was literally paralyzed by evil.

If he were to leave this world where he'd seen evil and return to that other world that seemed to be without evil, what would change?... Everyone there consumes (and will continue to consume—and he as well) the products of evil. The heart of the matter was more profound than the question of leaving or not leaving. There was nowhere to go. After he'd watched those good workers with the electric goads and seen the streams of yellow sparks pouring from the calves' tongues, where could he go?... It would stay with him now wherever he went—his knowledge and his complicity.

He kept on working day after day. That's what happens. Not only had he seen Evil but Evil had seen him, seen him and said: there you are. It was as if something in him had broken. A voice inside would whisper his guilt to him. He was no longer able to ask Pops to let him go. He was not able to venture off into the steppe, not able to work out a deal with any of the workers at the plant.

Of course, if a helicopter were to notice his fire at night in the steppe and come and land next to him, the young man would rush to it in a flash, leap in and yell, "Let's go!"—he was up to that, that he could do. He would jump into the helicopter and shout, "Let's go!"—and they'd fly away. If they came—great, but they'd have to land by his bonfire by themselves, convince him it was all real—they themselves, the roar of the motor, and the hot air churned up by the rotor blade.

5

At first it's television that irritates Ilya Ivanovich—the stories of murders, dismemberments in hallways, babies stuffed in trash bins and other such crime details. Then he increasingly comes to dislike the countless alcoholics who burn to death in apartment fires of their own making. He gets mad. He's irritated. He doesn't want to know any of this anymore. From now on, no one in his home can watch TV, except for his wife, who watches after Ilya Ivanovich has gone to bed (but even then the sound is turned down as low as possible). He doesn't go to the movies either. Self-imposed restrictions can help for a time. But, needless to say, *it* is increasing anyway, increasing little by little by itself, and television and the movies have nothing to do with it.

Soon Ilya Ivanovich is beside himself whenever somebody is insulted on the streetcar, and he's totally unable to listen to the howls of a child who's been slapped in the face. (Maybe by his parents and maybe even for a reason.) And so it happens that one day Ilya stops going to see his friends. He also stops going for walks on the street. Only to and from work. But even on his regular everyday route he looks out the bus window and sees a kitten that was crushed by a car while clumsily, no doubt, crossing the street that night, or the remains of a pigeon—also conspicuously there, reduced to tatters with just a little head sticking up; don't you see, they flattened it completely, but the pigeon's little head sticks up and looks at you. No, he can't travel any more, he can't sit by the bus window until they remove the pigeon, wash away the remains with a hose, or until the rain comes ("Just think about it!" he told me. "Some people kill them and other people wash them away!"), he feels so bad that from this day on he can't ride to work, so he takes sick leave. He's at home now. He's only at home. Walking around inside the courtyard, never the streets. Needless to say, even in the building's courtyard where he walks a painful encounter lies in wait for him: suddenly he sees a broken bush. Yes, someone had broken off a branch. Or pulled out a bush by the roots. In essence, even grass was enough to stir his vulnerable soul—a broken blade of grass, oozing from the tear. Out of love, the friend of my youth Ilya, Ilya Ivanovich, can't take his eyes off this blade of grass; it hurts him, pains him so much that a cosmic whistle shrieks inside his ears, his heart beats and pounds, and along with the pain something is slowly squeezed out, drop by drop, wrung from his pounding heart. Like a yellow flare, his childhood suddenly flashes through his mind—one after another, bright sparks from a past summer; his tears begin to choke him, a terrible spasm blocks his throat, and... and then Ilya Ivanovich, my friend, a grown-up man, sets out briskly through the courtyard, cuts straight across the children's playground, then (even more hastily) rushes past the concrete strip by the entrance, faster, get home faster, he's trembling, all the way up the elevator—now he's finally in his apartment, he throws himself face down on the bed, buries his head in the pillow, and sobs.

Life, people, the surrounding world—*it* was at work.

Ilya Ivanovich's depressed; suddenly he's manic and then he's depressed again—he calls the clinic, where they know him quite well and aren't surprised by his call at all, but they just ask him to stay at home and be patient for another day or two until there's a free spot in his usual ward. Naturally, if it becomes acute and too painful, they'll find a place for him in some other ward right away. Do you want to come now?... No, no. He'll be all right for a day or so. Thank you... He made the call. He feels better. He'll be protected during the difficult days that are coming. His psyche is back at its job.

He calls me in the evening. Or else some Vitaly Sergeyevich, another friend of his. He just wants to talk a little, have a conversation with me; now that he feels protected for a while, Ilya Ivanovich can talk about life in general and about our difficult world. Yes, just talk a little. Now that he's going away, he's not afraid, his sharpness of mind returns as well as his sense of irony about himself.

"Will you go with me to the looney bin?" He doesn't like his relatives to go to the hospital with him. He thinks that if relatives take you it just means lots of tears and trouble. He won't consider his illness something very dangerous—it's just my nerves, they've gotten a little worse. *My poor head needs a bit of care again.* And that's it. If a friend goes with him to the hospital, it's obvious that it's not so momentous and alarming an event.

After a day or so we're on our familiar road, circling around the district's sixteen-story tower. The hospital is on the outskirts of the city. Set behind a fence, a proper fence, it had been converted from a former monastery (given a new look). In any case, as we approach it, and we always walk at a leisurely pace, sharing the load–he with two small bags and I with a large one (clothes and a supply of juices), I see a well-protected institution–the psychiatric hospital. From the distance it looks like a fortress in which a vulnerable human being can seek shelter from the evil that inundates our world.

What a reversal! (and by the same token–what a distance, what a long road). If that young man from the future who invented the ATm-241 had travelled the land and flown on airplanes over vast spaces abounding in peace, and had found evil that was contained (penned-in, hidden behind walls), then my friend Ilya Ivanovich, a real person of our time, from the vast world abounding in evil, found only a stretch of land acceptable for himself, a strip of space behind the walls of a hospital. A small strip free of evil. There Ilya Ivanovich took refuge, safeguarded by tranquilizers and the psychotherapy of the benevolent doctors who treated him.

To the young inventor from the future, evil appeared to be isolated within an enclosed piece of steppe, and in this steppe they only killed animals (no small evil, but limited and enclosed behind a fence). Thus, one could try to imagine the future world in concert with him–what an earthly miracle it was, that is (well, apart from certain strips of enclosed exceptions), what kind of life they must have in places where radiant people travel freely, flying here and there, where there have been no wars or murders for ages and, in general, these radiant-faced men and women just flutter about, they flutter like doves, and do their work and invent assemblies, fight for various reasons or for no reason, but evil–doesn't exist.

We come closer; we can see the envisaged stretch of the hospital walls and their buttresses as well–old towers. A fenced off and also well-guarded strip of happiness. The towers (also part of the monastery, in the past, of course) are especially impressive. We've seen many invaders, they say. We held our ground. And we'll hold our ground now.

A fortress. The friend of my youth, Ilya Ivanovich, would like his frazzled "I" to be protected and safely enclosed behind these fortress walls as well as behind the walls of medicines and qualified doctors and the daily regimen. (No, there's no "WELCOME" on the gates.) At the hospital entrance Ilya tells me good-bye. He doesn't want to prolong the walk even a bit, since he's a little scared of himself, he's afraid to be outside these walls and anyway he's waited so patiently and on edge these two days for his place in the ward to be free. It's time for him to go.

We squeeze each other's hand. Bye. For at least six weeks, he says.

His dining room in the hospital doesn't offer a meat course (that's all he'd need to go over the edge). Many mentally disturbed patients aren't in any condition to see even a modest burger—every piece of meat begins its journey at the slaughterhouse. Therefore, a special menu is devised for some of the hospital wards. Ilya Ivanovich is in one of these. Cereal, milk, cottage cheese. Vegetable soups. Relatives provide juice and fruit if they can.

"Do you think they're just hiding the meat and the ground-up stuff from me and my neighbors in the ward? Or is it forbidden in the entire hospital?"

Since he's already adapted himself to the place, he wants to think that there aren't even secondary signs of evil or worldly malice behind the hospital walls. He wants to think that his fortress is just that.

"I've heard the food in this hospital is vegetarian and dairy products," I say cautiously.

"Where did you hear that?"

His voice sounds impatient, and I realize he wants to be deceived. And I deceive him.

"I heard the doctor talking to the dietician."

"Aha. I see."

That was good enough.

He and I talked a lot about the nature of evil and the various ways malice manifests itself. Perhaps Ilya's inner nervousness was externalized this way, emerging in his sometimes nervous conversation. Once I told him that when I was still an adolescent I'd discovered (or correctly guessed) that evil never ends. Evil extends (and is mutable) in time rather than space. And when I asked him in turn, "Ilya, when do you think you found out that evil exists and has no end—*that evil lives,*" he answered, "Believe it or not, I've always known."

"From childhood?"

"Yes, from childhood. Even earlier. Always."

But he didn't want to talk about how he knew (or sensed) it.

I asked if that knowledge was connected to the fact he's half-Jewish. (It wasn't a tactless question, Ilya knew me well, he'd known me forever. The question wasn't meant to be very penetrating—it was rather general. And as everyone knows—it's no secret—these days Ilya Ivanovich might himself have been a victim of inter-ethnic hostility. Especially on the streets. Standing in lines. In the bus. In a crowd.)

"No," he said, after thinking it over. "It's not connected... My half-Jewish half-Russianness has only confirmed what I've always known."

He thought about it a while longer, then sadly repeated, "Always."

One time he was in the vice-principal's office (something to do with his son, who was then a tenth grader), and a television was on, whether it was in that office or some other, I don't know. And during their conversation, the typical conversation between a school administrator and the parent of a student, the television just had to start talking about the poor working conditions that exist in our meat plants. Right then and there they played a clip about a slaughterhouse. No one's putting any money into it, they said. The equipment's obsolete! They showed the animals just as the current was about to be switched on. The cocked muzzles of the cows in cramped boxes. Their moos (both the sound and a quick shot. About five seconds' worth. Just so that the commentary on the screen would seem substantive and specific). Ilya Ivanovich paled. He grasped his chest suddenly, as if he'd been stabbed. Then he jumped up and ran out into the hall. The director decided he'd gotten sick from the stuffy air. In the hall Ilya Ivanovich stood near a wastebasket and puked, he unloaded everything and then—without even washing up in the school bathroom—rushed home. He ran along the street with his jacket flung wide open and his tie askew (for school visits it was customary to wear proper and respectable clothes), a balding forty-eight year old man with shaking lips and a spattered chin—he ran and occasionally cried out as if some sharp pain was shooting through him. He ran into his apartment and collapsed face down on the bed as he always did on such occasions, so as to release the tide of emotions. But this time things didn't turn out well—he had his first heart attack.

When you hear on the radio or read in the paper that the author (of the news report) feels terrible because of a poisoned pike-perch that flung itself belly up on the shore and is lying there covered with black oil, or when the subject is an oak tree that's been cut down for a new housing project and how terrible and painful such an action is (it was of mythic proportions and gave such shade in the heat), you can't help but think that you don't believe it, at least not very much. Painful? Do we really feel pain? Ilya Ivanovich, my friend from youth, did feel real pain on account of the pike and the oak. But we don't feel pain—we feel sorry.

A year later he died at home from a second heart attack. On a night when the moon was out for everyone.

* * *

Once Ilya stopped liking me because he remembered that I go fishing every summer. "Do you tear the hook out of the fish's innards?" he asked.

I answered that it happens quickly and in the heat of the catch. You haul in the fish on the end of the line and pull out the hook. It's all very quick.

He asked, "And do you ever think about what it would be like to be on a hook? To swallow it and then not be able to spit it out or pull it out or hawk it up? They drag you in and then they tear the hook out of you, how would you like that?"

I painstakingly explained (I didn't yet understand him completely then) that with pike, say, in order to lessen the suffering of the fish, and also just not to mess oneself up with the blood, which sometimes is quite plentiful (and mainly in order to make things go faster—since you have to keep on fishing, because when they're biting every moment is dear and you can't just stand there and gape), for all these reasons the hook is removed with the help of an extractor. And at that moment something made me explain how there's a delicate fork that fans out at the end and how it's lowered into the fish's gullet along the line and hook that the fish has swallowed, how it's pushed into the innards little by little until it frees the hook. Ilya started to feel ill. But he kept still. He was in one of those phases when he could still tolerate the evil of the surrounding world to a certain degree. He didn't become sick, he didn't leave or scream, he just said, "That's enough"—but he didn't forget.

And for almost half a year, whenever I phoned him, I'd hear a poor imitation of his son's voice say that he, Ilya Ivanovich, was not at home.

He receives good treatment in the hospital, he explained (they "numb the soul"), and each time he returns from the looney bin he feels the pain of the living and dying less acutely. He feels he's a warrior. He even feels he has the ability to wage the eternal war of the living with the living—and that means to live. He spoke the word "warrior" with irony, of course. Maybe the ancient word at such a moment seemed to him almost synonymous with the word "killer."

"Yes," Ilya said, "when I come out of the hospital and leave the wall and towers behind, I feel like a warrior. And I'm alive."

I remember thinking then that we, the living, are all warriors.

I remembered there was a very well-known, wise Tibetan lama who swept or had someone sweep away the dust in front of his feet so that not a single footstep of his could accidentally squash a bug crawling across his path. The lama even breathed through a gauze mask so as not to kill any microbes stuck to the mucous membrane that might die when he inhaled.

The lama felt himself to be a warrior—that's for sure. But he wanted to be a coward, a cowardly warrior who would run from the field of battle without killing or wounding anyone.

It crossed my mind that the microbes probably also felt they were warriors, but they were courageous, ready to perish in great numbers and in unequal battle—to die, perhaps, even while infecting the lama with some disease. But the gauze over his dry mouth was like the United Nations.

In essence, the lama and the microbes were really all warriors in a common battle. For they were alive.

In fact, we've always killed. And it's simply amazing that we warriors have still not gobbled each other up—or gobbled ourselves up. Something protects us. The swallow's saliva which glues the nest together. Something rocks us in our enormous child's cradle, and sings to us that we are people, people, people. What is it? Or who is it who protects us?

Right after our conversation about what or who is protecting people, I saw ahead of us, on a street with two-way traffic, a pigeon that had been squashed by a car. It had been stamped right onto the asphalt together with its beak and its tiny feet. And only a little bit of the down being scattered by a breeze rose up into the air as a reminder that at one time the flattened pigeon had had a three-dimensional form. If Ilya Ivanovich (and he was walking right beside me) had seen the down floating in the air, he'd have had a nervous breakdown. Ilya wouldn't have wanted to live while the flattened pigeon was lying there and people just walked by and cars drove on and life continued. When the traffic slowed, some other pigeons flew down briefly to see the one that had been stamped onto the pavement; not fully understanding what had happened to their friend, they landed, took a look, and flew off again when they heard the noise of oncoming cars—the instruments of fate. And over the squashed creature lies only the down of its small body, light bits of fluff in the breeze. The down *billows* above the body just as dove-gray fog billows over a lake in the morning.

Ilya Ivanovich had seen it even before I did—naturally, even before. He'd even winced with pain for a moment, then the wrinkles on his brow smoothed out, the pain passed, slid off his face. He started swallowing the lump in his throat, as if he were choking on food. He started to rub his temples. But he calmed down. We'd walked about a hundred meters by then and Ilya Ivanovich kept on repeating that everything was fine, he'd hold up—these days he was in good shape.

Another time he would simply have ended the walk, stopped the conversation mid-sentence and headed home. He'd have gone to bed and stayed there, clasping his head in his hands and quietly moaning, "Nnnn! Nnnn!"

Although they live together, Ilya Ivanovich is divorced from his wife. His wife truly treats him well, she looks after him, remembers his diet, and if he's in bad shape she calls the doctors at his request and sits by his side at night, holding his hand while he dozes. But all the same she's divorced from him; they separated when the symptoms of his illness had become very acute and his wife didn't understand what was wrong with him. And she divorced him out of fear, because he'd forbidden her to eat so many things, forbidden her to cook meat and fish, and he'd grabbed the knife right out of her hand, and so forth and so on. Since the divorce he's lived in his own room. And his wife and their grown son live in two other rooms in the very same apartment.

The son's not there now, by the way. He's in the army, in a tank unit. Their son is a first-year student at the institute and if the parents had taken the trouble to get some kind of certificate, they could have had his military service deferred or even gotten him excused from it completely. But the wife, who was afraid that her son's mental state might follow the pattern of the father's, sought advice from doctors who apparently decided that considering his heredity it would be more helpful for the boy (keeping his future in mind) to do his military service and partake in a little physical work in the fresh air, and so it was that he became a tanker.

Ilya Ivanovich choked on his words and started to protest–what if his son was sent to Afghanistan, where he might be killed and where he'd have to kill? But they assured him that this group of draftees wouldn't be sent to Afghanistan, besides the young man had light-colored hair, light brown hair to his shoulders, and the ones with light hair are never sent to that hell, because they've become special targets there. (A widely-held opinion of those years.)

And so Ilya Ivanovich sadly kept silent. He let himself be deceived and comforted–what else could he have done in his condition? And, as a matter of fact, his son wasn't sent to Afghanistan.

When we were introduced, Ilya Ivanovich's wife extended her hand and said her name quickly, "Olya."

Ilya Ivanovich's wife was having an affair with a doctor from the district hospital. When Ilya's illness became more acute and for the first time there was talk of hospitalization, his wife ran around from doctor to doctor for months on end, trying to do something, leaving no stone unturned, making every effort on his behalf. It was then that her feeling for one of the doctors developed (opportunity doesn't wait)—it developed and continues to this day. Olya is an honest woman, and she's not able to hide things well, you can see she feels ashamed. And Ilya Ivanovich is incurably ill—it's a hard weight to bear.

The doctors' diagnosis was definite—schizophrenia. There's a nicety here, however—the doctors consider Ilya Ivanovich ill and therefore unable to bear the cruelty of the world in which he lives. (In which we all live—but we're all right!) They insist that the illness came first and the vulnerability was a consequence.

Keeping to the theme of killing, which was always on Ilya Ivanovich's mind, one time I mentioned to him that I had imagined a young man from a future time when there would no longer be wars or killing in everyday life and when cows would be slaughtered for meat in abattoirs that were hidden and kept secret somewhere in the steppes, like concentration camps. The young man, who is quite ambitious, would be sent on a special assignment to improve the technology there (he won't suspect that there's an ordinary slaughterhouse two steps away from him). I gave him a quick description of the plant and proving ground on the other side of the wall and said that all the conversations there would revolve around science and new technology, new technology and science.

Ilya suddenly became interested in something completely different, "You're lucky. You know how to get rid of whatever torments you!"

I objected, "I don't get rid of it at all that way; on the contrary, I become even more involved in it."

"Exactly!" he shouted fervently. "You become even more involved and you see *it* from within. And from inside it's not painful."

He gave a quick laugh, "What a clever guy!"

I saw his point. And, trying to define it more precisely, I asked, "Are you saying that we empathize so as not to feel pain? We empathize so as to become deeply involved and almost one with a person who's in pain—all to avoid seeing his pain from the outside?"

But at this moment Ilya was not open to dialogue. His thoughts had already wandered far off into the distance (I soon understood where), leaving not only my logic behind but that of our whole world, it seemed. He was silent.

After being silent for several minutes he said, "Listen. Make me a present of this subject."

"What do you mean?"

"Give it to me!"

I didn't understand.

He turned to me (we were walking on the left side, the shady side of their street) and as he spoke he looked me straight in the eye, "Give it to me. Give me this time, this meat plant, their fence, the high wall with the 'welcome.' Give me that young fellow, his ignorance, and then his realization. Give me the steppe, the stars, the smells!"

Remembering that Ilya, Ilya Ivanovich, the friend of my youth, had an incurable mental illness, I quietly answered, "Take it."

And he immediately fell into a long silence, maybe because he hadn't expected to get it so easily.

About a week later Ilya Ivanovich told me he'd been there. "Where?" I asked. "There."

That's right, he'd made his way to that proving ground in the steppe (in thought, needless to say), where he lay down in the thick and wild hemp at the very foot of the wall, and he was dazed by the smell there. When it got dark, he climbed over the wall. Leapt as he had when young. Indeed, the wall wasn't well guarded. It was easy for

Ilya Ivanovich to walk around the inner grounds, a guard shouted something to him once. But that was all.

It was a moonlit night. You could see very clearly. Not far from the outside wall a small light shone in the guest house (the second house was still empty) where the young man on assignment worked late into the night, his eyes glued to the screen, while he counted the seconds lost, or, from an opposite point of view, gained, on the conveyor line. The conveyor that he'd discovered on his very first work assignment and that he couldn't get away from. All of us find such a conveyor sooner or later. And his assembly. Yes, exactly, and Raphael pursued this, too—an art that paints and allays suffering, and isn't art also an assembly with a state-of-the-art design? Ilya Ivanovich moved closer to the small house and glanced in the window with some caution—the man on assignment was working. The computer screen was brightly lit. Just imagine, in order to stay calm while counting up seconds, this young technocrat was letting the videotape play the disassembly of the cows in reverse. The conveyor was there, but it ran backwards. (Ilya forgot that I'd told him this detail—he was convinced he'd seen it. Maybe he saw it *too*). Just imagine, no sympathizing—the seconds tick away and you're able to count them.

Yes, in reverse, out of pieces of meat, a spine, and skin you get a live cow. She stands there and looks at you. Her large brown eyes blink. Do *these* eyes (that is, the ones restored by the reversed tape) remember their calf, the meadow, and the five chamomile plants scattered in the grass?... The cow stands and switches her tail. And a ray of sun shines on her flank and her back. (Is it the same ray? That's the question.) And a bumblebee that had by chance flown into the frame circles around, intoxicated by the sun.

"He's just acting foolish. Sitting there and playing games with the video—back and forth," I said with some jealousy. (Who knows my young man on assignment better than I?)

I explained, "At first he killed (participated in killing) and now he's resurrecting. Maybe this is the way art is born. The desire to play things over again even though life is finished."

Ilya Ivanovich gave a laugh. "Playing games? Not a chance! Believe me: he counted the seconds. Simply and coldly counted them up in competition with the computer."

Ilya Ivanovich was certain that the life in the manufacturing plant and proving ground was his now since, after all, *that* was what I gave him. Maybe it was. He spoke quickly and confidently and with detailed knowledge about the life there. He would talk about the women who washed the cows. He saw them at work, young women in scarves. They came when the fine jets were pounding the sides of the cows. Ablution. It wasn't so easy to recognize a woman there, you know how much a scarf can change a face... But then he became better acquainted with the women, he went to one of their homes as a guest, a tidy little house, there were flowers in the front garden. No, no sunflowers. The volunteers? Yes, he'd seen them. Strong workmen, who drink, but in moderation. They have aged and calloused hands. In the evenings they sang. They invited Ilya Ivanovich to be their guest. They sat in the moonlight...

"I love the moon at night," Ilya Ivanovich finished with a smile and not without a little irony. (As if guiding his listener back to reality after a story about a fantastic journey.)

And switching back to the style of the present (one which people use to discuss a movie plot) he conjectured, "Haven't you thought about the fact that maybe they won't let him leave now? No, I don't mean the ones who work in the plant. But the ones who live in the outside world (and seemingly know nothing at all about the slaughterhouses). They won't let him come back. They're not sending anyone after him. They're exactly the ones. Why let another person who has recognized evil into their world?"

And he grinned, "What good would he bring to the world?"

* * *

A moonlit night. And the wall. And the fact that Ilya Ivanovich leapt over it easily. Maybe he wanted to return to the time when we were young. (When he was still healthy, even though vulnerable. The vulnerability was there before the illness.) Sometimes we'd forget to take our student cards with us and when we returned to the dormitory, in order to avoid a squabble with the old porter, we'd just leap over the fence. Even in daytime. In bright sunlight.

A man assimilates the murder of homeless dogs, that is, the killing becomes part of Man, of his very mien. It's in him even if he never thinks about it and doesn't once remember it during his life.

And what's so amazing about the fact that we kill in street fights or in the normal surroundings of our homes, that we do violence, dismember corpses, and wage war from time to time. For that's who we are. Neither in our ethics nor in our consciousness is there a place for what is authentically ours. One ought not to kick a cat or beat a dog, but it's all right to annihilate a hundred and thirty-two thousand two hundred and seventy cats by electric shock (the yearly statistics from one city). That's what we're like.

And this is the world we live in.

...Ilya Ivanovich's wife. She said "Olya" so quickly and extended her hand–no last name or patronymic. So that she could be tough ahead of time, in case I suddenly found out or heard something (or maybe I already knew) about the doctor with whom she was having the long affair. Straightforward. And she said something to Ilya about food. Also with a suppressed hardness in her voice, even though she spoke quietly. About vegetable soup probably. Not manna from heaven. "Doesn't it hurt the cabbage?" she asked. But she asked it kindly because Ilya smiled. His eyes even sparkled, which meant he appreciated her humor.

Meaning, You and I. The Denisieva cycle.* "Here is the world where you and I lived." And then—"my angel," spoken like *myangel.* A single tone. Did Tolstoy like Tyutchev? The death of Ivan Ilyich.**

6

As soon as the corner tower of the psychiatric hospital comes into view we both undergo a change. We're already different people. I'm relieved that we're here, we've arrived and nothing (from the point of view of the escort) happened on the way to irritate Ilya. Ilya Ivanovich is also relieved—these walls and these towers are like the pill he took, which he swallowed with a little water, and it's already in his stomach and beginning to take effect. It's so nice to unload his burdens onto the shoulders of a pill. The pill is a tower. The upper part of the tower nearest us has fallen in.

"Did you ever notice that tower is odd?" I ask and point it out with one hand (the other hand holds the large bag).

"It's old," he answered.

Ilya Ivanovich asked me to go to his apartment and find some notebook that had a schedule of the medicines he took. He said that he absolutely must compare records and it was important. I think that his engineer's mind simply

*A cycle of poems written by the poet Fyodor Tyutchev (1803-73), who was involved in a scandalous affair with Yelena Denisieva, his daughter's governess. The cycle was written after her death in 1864 and contains some of the best-known tragic love poems in Russian. The lines cited are from the poem "On the Eve of the Anniversary 4 August 1864" (1865) [*tr.*].

**The title of one of Lev Tolstoy's late stories about the changes a man undergoes in the face of death. Ivan Ilyich learns about faith and love from the simple servant who tends to him in his final days. His name and patronymic in reverse form the name Ilya Ivanovich, the friend of the narrator here [*tr.*].

demanded some kind of food for analysis. It was late in the evening—I took his request to his wife and she understood at once (she was already used to understanding his requests), led me to his room and said, "Go ahead, please search." I searched but didn't find anything. Ilya had given me several contradictory instructions—search "there" and if it's not there, then "there" and or perhaps "there." I poked around all the "theres," looked here and looked there, and trampled around his narrow room without much enthusiasm. When his wife looked in (Olya twice invited me to have a cup of tea), I answered, "No, thanks. I don't want any."

Although tired from the search, I set out for the kitchen anyway and drank the tea and his wife took my place and walked around the narrow room searching for it—also futilely. While Olya was serving tea, she talked with me in just as restrained a manner as ever and about nothing in particular. She just smiled and showed me a letter her son the tanker had sent.

The phone rang and she spoke with the doctor she'd been close to for more than a year now. She spoke in the kind of voice that almost immediately reveals an intimate relationship between two people.

I sat and drank my cup of tea.

I couldn't tell Ilya Ivanovich that I hadn't found his notebook or the book he needed. He isn't able to accept an explanation as a fact, and my retelling of "it isn't there" and "it's not there either" and "I pulled out all the drawers two times" would only evoke his sympathy. He'd immediately begin to look over everything again (mentally travelling to the apartment) and search in all the places he'd pointed out to me. He'd look for the notebook in each of the three places. And, of course, he might fall into a rage and start asking to go home from the hospital, order a taxi even before the doctors had made their rounds and ask the head nurse to take his hospital gown and give him back his suit... So after the tea, as if with a new charge of energy, I returned to his room and searched. I looked in books. Crawled under the couch. Tried moving the wardrobe a little to the side, groped around in a spiderweb, looked inside a record cover and... there it was.

As instructed, I turned out the light in his room as I was leaving, and immediately caught sight of the moon in the window. Clutching the notebook in my hand, I stared into the flowing light. I thought about Ilya Ivanovich—the moonlight was in *his* window, it was for him. A lyrical moment had escaped from the everyday (liberated in the form of light). In the hospital he trusted in pills and doctors and the strong walls around him, but at the same time a silver light had come to him here. This soft glow addressed to Ilya Ivanovich absorbed my soul. It was *his* light, belonging to him, maybe it's his healing. And maybe he sees it there now, he's been given something in reserve—both here and there, I thought.

Ilya Ivanovich asked the doctors for permission to go home for a few days, assuring them that he felt quite well.

"Are you really feeling better, Ilya?" his alarmed wife asked him. (She sensed his health and illness better than others.)

"No," he answered her (already at home). "But I want to be here. I want to be with you. I want to go outside on the street. I'll try to go to work again..."

"Isn't it dangerous?"

"I want it so much," he answered, a bit belligerently, even.

His wife, relating this to me, used precisely this word—"belligerently."

Maybe once alone with himself, Ilya Ivanovich decided to be (and to die?) where we all were. His death came on either the second or third night after his return.

I didn't know about his return. I decided that he'd died in the hospital and that it was a happy, perhaps easy, death. He'd died isolated from evil because the doctors were protecting him, and even if he'd died in his sleep in the ward, evil wouldn't have been present there—the medication regulated his sleep and the intensity of his dreams.

I thought that because he didn't want to partake in evil, he'd chosen to die in this way, in no particular state, neither a complicated, nor a simple one, neither a social setting, nor an ordinary one. He ate very simple food. Kasha. And milk. He didn't even want to accept a broken branch on the side of the road. And he didn't. Evil stayed off to the side.

That's what I thought. And then I learned that he'd come back on his own to die in our gutter. To us. To our beautiful and malicious world. He came back for no reason. To his wife. He simply came back. Here is the world where you and I lived.

To my mind, Ilya's return home is connected in some unclear way (it's not clear how—but it's certain) with the young man who invented the ATm-241 and his failure to return to the world he'd lived in before.

Under the spell of evil (of the slaughterhouse? of the ATm-241? of his participation?), he stayed on at the plant and works there.

...Or else evil also overtook Ilya Ivanovich behind his hospital walls when a robust male nurse thrashed some raving patient, who had thrown his excrement around and then rushed onto Ilya's floor—to "the quiet ones"; the door was open, no one had been watching, and then "That's enough of him!"—and the quick mini-scene. As if Ilya really needed that!

I had the feeling (though not on that night, on another one), that we can't hide from the rays of the moon. I turned over onto my other side in bed and closed my eyes—the moon was there anyway. I wrapped a soft towel around my head and lay down—the same thing. The moon was in my eyes.

I gave up and walked to the window. The moon was resolutely giving off light. The rays pressed down on my eyes and on the window panes, as if there was a definite message in the light they brought.

Some time after his death Ilya Ivanovich's wife asked for my help. At first she called and insisted that I come to her home, "No, no, believe me, I simply have to talk to you here, at our home. Please come," and when I arrived she showed me a whole collection of Ilya Ivanovich's clothes in the wardrobe and asked me to take everything to a second-hand store. She opened the doors of a second wardrobe—I'd been called to look, as well as listen. There weren't so many clothes in here, but, still, a considerable number of things—a suit, two jackets, two separate pairs of trousers, jeans, several snow-white shirts, everything that our engineer had. Ilya Ivanovich had spent most of the past four years either in a hospital gown or at home in a warm house sweater. He hadn't worn his clothes, they were in perfect condition. And naturally I understood that what was left had to bring in quite a bit of money, since the *chief* bread-winner, as they said in the old days, was dead.

I didn't want to go to those dealers. I understood completely why their son, whose shoulders were much broader than Ilya's, wouldn't wear the "junk" or take it in to the resale stores. He'd left his tank and come home for ten days for the funeral. He had enough worries. I understood that too. And it would have been unpleasant to think that during these ten days the son had to take his father's things to the second-hand stores, even if he took them quietly, even if sullenly. But the son had left now and his wife, in my view, could do this job by herself some time later. If his wife, or former wife, had decided the dead man's things should go to a store, she should have been able to take them there herself, to run her warm hand one last time over the sleeves of his clothes and the smooth insides of his pockets. (That's what I thought–no rules exist and only an inner feeling indistinctly whispers something to us in every such instance.) But as soon as I breathed a word to the effect that I didn't want to go to the dealers either, she screamed, "How can you!" and she rushed out the door of his room, full of anger and pain.

Maybe I'd made a blunder. Maybe she also had some vulnerability that I hadn't divined. Such is life.

So I agreed. To be more precise, as soon as I heard her scream I knew I'd agree. I sat face to face with his wardrobe, one door of which was flung open, and focused every so often on the sleeves of a jacket and the shirts that hung side by side. I sat there a while, sighed, and reluctantly moved closer. The small wardrobe with his trousers and jeans was there too.

I gathered everything up in one pile and wanted to throw it all on the couch. But I thought again, I must try to be calm. I hung it all up again. And began to take things out on hangers, "little shoulders," as people here once said; I'd take something out, twirl it around on the hanger, appraise its worth, and if I thought that it was good enough for the second-hand dealers–approximately, of course; how could I price it!–I'd put it down on the couch.

I heard her steps in their kitchen and the sound of water running–maybe into the teakettle for tea, or maybe into a glass to quiet her nerves. I sensed that she wouldn't come in here now, that I should go and apologize, and say that I would agree to go.

I knew I'd apologize, there was nothing else I could do now, but for a long time I tried to overcome something in myself. While looking through his things I tried to see him. For the last time. I remembered that he usually wore that suit and that tie when he got ready to go to the school to see about his son's lessons. But where had I seen him in that windbreaker? Oh, yes! At their home, playing chess! In this shirt (or one like it) he'd go out on the balcony to smoke. Replaying the tape, I slowly accumulated the living person, reconstituting his life piece by piece as much as I could with the help of jackets and trousers and shirts. For a time, right here in this room in which he'd lived, Ilya Ivanovich began to move, he came close, he laughed. His eyes sparkled.

Their dark-gold color disappeared and the cleaned half-carcasses turned whiter and whiter as they returned from nonexistence (from the smoke house). And then, jumping through the saw with a backwards flash, the carcass reunited itself from its separated parts. In a fraction of a second it became a single piece. Whole. And immediately, skilled human hands swiftly began to stuff it: the lungs, a pair of kidneys, a stomach, intestines, an enormous liver were shoved in, and a heart flew even more rapidly into place. All the organs took their spots with an amazing precision, solidly, without the least urging and with no sensation of being cramped—everything was in its place. When the carcass was completely full, it dove into a stall, where it was rather quickly dressed. Just as a young man pulls on a pair of tight pants, or, more precisely, a jump suit, while lying back, so, or practically so, was the cow's own skin, which had flown down from somewhere above the video-screen, pulled over the naked carcass. And in strict correspondence with the law (the law of reverse motion) the registration stamp on the carcass instantly evaporated, vanished into the air, and the warm, live steam of the carcass, which had surrounded it in a mist, was drawn completely under the skin right before one's eyes.

"Minus two seconds. Correct?" Pops half stated, half asked.

"We're checking that now. Yes, two. Two, or almost three..."

A cow's head appeared, tossed from below like a ball—here, catch! During the course of flight it succeeded in acquiring cheeks and lips, stuffed itself once again with thick chunks of brain, and suddenly froze with a vacant look—in one fell swoop a pair of eyes stuck themselves in the holes. The next head flew up—and another pair of eyes. Followed by a universal granting of vision: the eyes recovered their sight. But by now the first head had crawled to the very edge of the conveyor where it suddenly took off and flew to the carcass. A man in overalls managed to make an incision, showing the head how to make its dive and where to attach itself. And the cow's head completed the maneuver with uncanny accuracy. It fused with the body.

"Plus one second"—the voice of Pops.

And the voice of the technical engineer who was checking on his computer, "Plus one and a half."

At the troughs blood flowed in reverse, the body of each cow was pumped full. Not a single drop was allowed to remain in the trough. The final stream, which absorbed the last red spatters and smudges, crept back into their veins, while simultaneously, with a sharp backwards movement of the blade, the tissue closed up cleanly—without a stitch. And the upside-down cows took off in a backwards procession, still hanging on their chains; with their bodies intact again, the cows sailed off one after another: the reflected herd departed on a still unknown road.

They began their ascent to the second floor (at the moment when the floor dropped beneath them). They ascended, flying up on sloping planks until the planks closed beneath them, the floor became horizontal, and all the cows lay down on the absolutely horizontal surface, all without exception; and only then did the electric dance of their resurrection begin. Like a whirlwind. Leaps, tumultuous bodies, a convulsive dance of the resurrected, then a flight a meter or two high in the air, and broken front and hind legs begin to mend, the slain bodies regain their stance, a shaking of horns, then bellows, bellows!—and quiet. Quiet. A slow stir and the cows stood side by side, arranged in rows, scarcely brushing against each other. Within a flash of a second they had acquired life and, with life, came order again. That's the only way they can live on earth. Life is given back to them. And the man in the yellow overalls, with one strap across the shoulder, moves slowly away from the switch. He takes his hand off the knife switch's handle. But his hand is still extended, as if directed overhead—the man-leader is hailing the cows on their newly begun life.

And right away the folding door of the box slides open and the simultaneously revived cows slowly exit backwards out of the boxes, backing up further and further, with the very same humility in their round eyes that was there when they had moved forward into the slaughter.

This group of Burenkas had managed to grow horns . And ears. I skipped over that, the man on assignment thought. Now he'd have to display the side conveyor on the left side of the screen and track it again. The seconds that can be lost at the conveyor's junctions are especially important (and hard to control). OK, here's the washing...

Washing, but clearly with the opposite effect: the more effervescent the water and the more iridescent and clean the fine jets hitting the cows' sides and ribs and flying over the horns to form fountains, the more the dung on the cement floor and the dirt and dust from the road returned to the cows' sides and the brittle straw and leaves of grass clung to the sides and udders. The young women wearing scarves stroked the cows with a backward movement of their hands, as if against the coat, but gently, in a nice way, a human way.

And then, with their rumps bumping into each other, the cows backed out along the cement chutes and entered the stockyard. Forgotten obscenities rang out, distorted and spoken backwards. There came a "Tig! Ti-i-ig!" ("Git! Gi-i-it!"—the sound track was rewinding too) and the resuscitated cows moved apart to gradually subsiding cries and curses. They chewed the grass that was scattered around them, rays of sunlight lay on their sides, a bumblebee flew by; this was *life,* and the video imparted the great lie that mankind can create the living even as he destroys it. The quality of the picture was first-rate; a running caption indicated that a countdown in seconds was about to begin: the creation of the world.

7

A person cannot be considered to be left behind until he's tried to leave.

In the steppe, old shrubs are a great help, even if they grow thinly. The wall enclosing the plant was far behind him now and the man on assignment had wandered deeper into the steppe. It was a night like any other. He quickly looked for a dry shrub, one that was strong and thin, and he chopped it down (with a small axe he had grabbed), and cut it up into small pieces. The bonfire caught. It began to crackle. The man on assignment moved a few steps away from the heat and looked up at the dark sky, searching among the cooled fires of stars for the moving fiery dot of a helicopter flying past. A reddish-yellow bee, he thought, remembering the cow in the stockyard that had come back to life on the screen.

He'd have to gird himself with patience now. There was no sense in scanning the sky every minute. As he moved off to the side a little, wearily pacing back and forth, the man on assignment happened to cast a glance beyond the shrub off to the left, and there he caught sight of a fire that was as stationary as his own. Without a doubt the light was from another bonfire. He shuddered–it wasn't very far from him. Maybe he had a colleague out here (or maybe it was some kind of security force?). He thought about it for a minute. Naturally, his fire would have been spotted too. It was worth taking the chance, then, and going to see... He started out. He took a roundabout way across the steppe and got closer, very carefully at first, then more boldly. Just one man was sitting by the fire, it wasn't a guard.

The man on assignment walked up, said hello, and gave his name. The man at the fire spoke his name too. Yes, he'd also been sent here on assignment, he'd lived in a small guest house behind the wall on the plant grounds, only he'd been on the eastern side. They were almost the same age, they'd both come here from the capital–their fates were remarkably similar, the only substantial difference was that his colleague had been here a long time, for about half a year...

"Are you hoping that someone will fly by here too?" asked the young man on assignment.

"Yes. Of course. What else is there to hope for?" the other man answered.

The young man on assignment asked if there hadn't been at least one helicopter during the half year. The other shrugged his shoulders—how could one know? Some tiny lights had moved across the night sky. But they were rare. Then he said, "I'm not the only one waiting. Some have been waiting a year, even longer."

He pointed, "There. Look over there..."

Two more fires were visible in the distance.

The following night, after he'd kindled his fire and made sure it would burn steadily for a while, he set out in the direction of the other fires. It turned out that the fires belonged not only to men sent there on assignment, but also to workers from the plant whose jobs had begun to depress them. Among the fire-builders there was even one volunteer.

He spoke with them all about the same thing—their hope. With a persistence characteristic of someone new (newcomers always insist on uniting forces), the young man on assignment tried to bring them all together—wouldn't it be easier together, if all of them, stuck here by fate, so alike in their goals and hopes... wouldn't it be easier for them to build one colossal fire all together?... No, it seemed that it wouldn't. They convinced him. The very scattering of the fires could prompt the helicopter pilot to change his course a little and take an interest in what fires were burning at night and why. Whereas one fire is just a fire. Someone who had wandered off in the steppe might just be warming himself. No, everyone should build and light his own fire and keep it going and keep hoping. There were people here who'd already tried many different things and they'd been waiting for more than a year. You could believe them.

He was used to seeing the other small fires now, some close to his, some far away. He was used to hearing the sporadic calls of the steppe birds at night.

"Enjoy your dinner," he said, as he passed a fire where a stout man was sitting. He was a disillusioned volunteer from Section 2.

"Thanks. Sit down. My baked potatoes turned out well today."

The man on assignment sat down beside him and started to talk, "Aren't you bored here by yourself?"

"Bored? Not really. It's nice to look at the fire."

He frequently ran across a family man in the middle of the night, a man in a rush carrying a bundle of twigs. The man was on the way to light his fire and he was always late and he would yell at his wife who had overslept and hadn't woken him on time during the night. He had asked her to wake him up sooner! He had bad feet (he was one of the men who drove the cattle into the boxes—he drove bulls, and that's a lot different from cows! His feet had had decades' worth of trampling ahead of time!). But even with his bad feet he goes to light his fire.

The young man on assignment studied them all, but saw only one thing—people, ordinary people. They were simply waiting.

In general, they all had the same problem—they weren't able to break out of the system that their routine work at the plant had established for them. They couldn't restructure themselves. An unproductive segment. Nor were they able to trust in chance and venture further into the steppe.

But they were able to hope.

Some slept by their fires. That was understandable. They'd worked during the day, and if they were tired they couldn't sit for long by the fire at night—they'd get groggy and fall asleep. He recognized her even as she slept, though—she was dozing, wrapped in a shawl.

He woke Olya quietly, "Your fire's about to die and you're sleeping!"

She was happy to see him. She said she had some milk with her–would he like some?

"Do you also go out at night to make a fire?" he asked.

"Rarely. Sometimes..."

"But why?"

"I don't know. Everyone goes. So sometimes I have to go make a fire too."

One of the men who stunned the cattle was just getting ready to nap by his fire. His face was familiar from the videotape, where he could be seen jabbing the tongues of cows in the throes of death with an electric goad, after which the sparks shot out in clusters. We pay our dues. It's not easy work running around all day among the giant twitching carcasses.

"I thought you liked your work," he told the man.

The man wrapped himself more tightly in his sheepskin coat. He threw a branch onto the bonfire. And yawned.

"I used to like it at times," he answered.

"But later you wanted to leave?"

The man yawned again, "How can you leave! There's steppe in all directions..."

The man on assignment sat down by the fire. Sure, he was yawning. And he was tired. But he was waiting too.

And so his next encounter (after he met the man who stunned the cows, on the very same night) wasn't much of a surprise. As he got near, he saw a man doubled up next to a fire, shaking all over. The man had vomited and was surely ill.

"Throw on a few branches while I clear out my throat!" the man shouted with difficulty. He writhed in pain again, and coughed up bloody phlegm.

The man on assignment recognized the voice, and after the other had finished coughing and finally straightened up and sat facing him, the man on assignment was completely convinced that the wrinkled, stubborn face he saw was that of Pops. Naturally, he didn't have to ask about anything. He could have talked about the nighttime dampness, or just asked if he'd been coughing that way for long. But, after all, Pops had cared about production: he'd been so afraid that information would accidentally slip out or be leaked—and now he was making fires too.

The man on assignment said, "But why do you want to fly away? You know perfectly well that no matter where you go, you'll never be free of the cow heads crawling along the conveyor and pieces of beef from which the taste of blood has been thoroughly removed. People eat the same thing everywhere in the world."

Pops (wiping his face after coughing again) answered, "But what if we fly off to some other worlds? If suddenly there's oxygen somewhere else?"

With a wily laugh he added, "Nope! We must hope, we must always keep on hoping—the main thing is that the fire's burning and just you look at what a fine fire I've got!"

He spoke with pride. He really did have a good fire, but the brushwood hadn't been cut up and the whole place was a mess, boughs and charred pieces of wood were scattered all about.

"Nope!" he repeated. His eyes shone, "There's always hope."

The man on assignment asked, "And what if someone were to tell people the truth all the same, gather up the courage to speak—let people see themselves for just one brief moment? If you like, I'll take the chance myself. Let them declare me a madman. Let them put me in isolation. You can scream about me everywhere and proclaim me a slanderer and scoundrel! But while defaming me, you'll have to tell the true story nonetheless—won't that do some good, perhaps?"

"No. None at all," answered Pops with conviction.

"But why?"

Pops had completely recovered from his attack. He poked the coals in the fire. Rubbed his freezing hands. He sighed deeply, as if he were in his own home: "Oh, my boy! My dear boy."

* * *

The very number of people waiting was amazing. In the distance fires were scattered everywhere.

He asked a man at a fire, "Even so, what if we begin to consider things together? If only in order to obtain some kind of experience in waiting."

The other just shrugged his shoulders.

He asked again: "But do you see helicopter lights fly over?"

"Yes, but very far away."

"And only on clear nights?"

"Yes. You can't see anything if there's fog or even if it's dusk."

He asked about his neighbors. "Who's making a fire there?"

"I can't tell for sure. The old man, I think. I used to see him last year. The old man always makes his fire in the same place. Though it's in a slightly different spot now..."

"Maybe the old man died?"

"I doubt it. He builds his fire in a very particular way–I recognize that as his. The smoke always stays low. I wouldn't confuse it with the other fires."

But when the man on assignment came up to that fire, he saw a dead man, though it's possible he had only died a bit earlier. The low-smoking fire was still burning; it was dying out slowly, but it still burned. The dead man was lying off to one side, wrapped in a blanket. An unknown old man with absolutely gray hair. (He would probably have to report the death.)

Next to him were a canvas bag, some simple provisions, a supply of water in a flask–apparently he had been getting ready to move deeper into the steppe with his fire.

***

Until a certain moment the young man on assignment could not have imagined that there were so many people hoping and waiting. (That you would see so many bonfires in the middle of the night if you walked toward the shrubs.)

Now he understood that this was a whole world. He suddenly felt that he envied them terribly—not their fires, he had one too!—but the calm with which they sat at the fires. One might have thought that he, a young man, one who knew how to observe from the outside, would be the one with a sound mind, while they would be given to vain pursuits. But nothing is that simple. They are the ones who are calm. Oh, how calm they are compared with him! They are mighty, many, and calm.

On Reading Makanin

The heroes of both *Escape Hatch* and *The Long Road Ahead* are caught in terrifying situations–they face increasing isolation from the rest of humanity and must endure an agonizing wait for their struggle to end; yet there are significant differences between these works. Together, the texts, first published in 1991 in the journals *Novyi mir* and *Znamia,* provide a good introduction to Makanin's art, the meaning of which has been sharply debated over the years in Russia. Makanin likes to explore broad philosophical and social problems in his works, but gives his readers little direction on how he should be interpreted, a rather un-Russian feature which has left readers and critics puzzled. Over the course of his career Makanin gradually acquired the reputation of an enigmatic writer, strange, ironic, even cold–a consistently independent thinker who can't easily be fitted into any movement.

Vladimir Semyonovich Makanin was born in 1937 in Orsk, a city in the Urals. His father was a mining engineer and his mother a teacher of Russian. The steppe and mountains of the Urals often appear in his writing, and his love for music has a source there as well; he and his grandfather would regularly visit a small wooden church and listen to the singing. In 1954 Makanin went to Moscow to study mathematics; he graduated from Moscow University in 1960. His first book, published when he was twenty-seven, was on linear programming and weapons technology. A year later he published his first work of fiction, the novel *A Straight Line (Priamaia liniia,* 1965). In the same year, he left his career as a mathematician and enrolled in the State Institute of Cinematography, where he studied screenwriting and direction for two years. He wrote the screenplay for *A Straight Line,* which became a film in 1969.

It took Makanin a long time to capture the attention of the critics or the general public as a writer. Makanin is a contemporary of Andrei Bitov and Bella Akhmadulina, but his literary evolution is quite different. He remained in the background for most of the 60s and 70s. His works, for the most part stories and novellas, were published in books rather than in the literary journals where the most influential writers appeared. With the publication in 1979 of the short story "Klyucharyov and Alimushkin," he began to receive serious critical attention, and his novella about a folk healer, *The Forerunner (Predtecha,* 1983), was widely discussed, appearing at a time when the public was fascinated with non-traditional healing, hypnotists, psychics, and the like.

From the early 80s to the present, as the literary climate changed and Makanin came into his own as a writer, his reputation steadily grew both at home and abroad. Among his best works of the 1980s are *Antileader (Antilider,* 1980), *Left Behind (Otstavshii,* 1987),[1] *The Loss (Utrata,* 1987) and *A Man and A Woman, Odin i odna,* 1987). In 1991, the year the Soviet Union collapsed, the two works included here—*Escape Hatch (Laz)* and *The Long Road Ahead (Dolog nash put')*—were published, and *Escape Hatch* was named a finalist for the first Booker Russian novel prize in 1992. The following year Makanin won the prize for *Baize-covered Table with Decanter (Stol, pokrytyi suknom i s grafinom poseredine).* His new story "Prisoner of the Caucasus" ("Kavkazskii plennyi," 1995) is one of this year's literary sensations.

By the early 1980s Makanin had developed his own style of narration, which is characterized by a montage of plot fragments, dialogues, philosophical speculations, dreams and legends, often arranged with gaps in space and time. The stories take place in urban settings similar to Moscow and in a countryside like that of Makanin's youth. His characters tend to be types, average people in the circumstances of everyday life, and he generally does not individualize them with much physical detail or psychological complexity, preferring instead to show what one might call their nature or essence. Makanin often calls attention to the fictionality of his work: for instance, the hero in *The Long Road Ahead* is created by a character-narrator of another story.

The structures of *The Loss* and *Left Behind* are typical of Makanin's works in the 80s. *The Loss* contains three narratives that are interwoven in the montage pattern described above: one deals with a legend about a man who together with hired blind workers digs a tunnel beneath the Ural River; the second is a contemporary account of a man in a hospital who tries to help a young girl, perhaps in reality, perhaps in dream; in the third a man goes back to his native Urals on a private quest. Each story has a different narrator and takes place in a different time. The arrangement of the segments allows the reader to discover additional meaning in the text and it creates a model of a world that can be intuited by the principle of coincidence, or synchronicity, as Jung has described it: "The coincidence of events in space and time" is taken to mean "something more than mere chance, namely, a peculiar interdependence of objective events among themselves as well as with the subjective (psychic) states of the observer or observers."[2]

Left Behind also has three narratives: one takes place in the 1950s when a young writer follows a woman to the Urals, a time when people were returning from Stalin's prison camps; the second occurs in the present and involves relations between the hero of the first narrative and his father, who is mentally disturbed; the third takes place in the remote past and tells the story of a retarded child who is exploited by a group of miners because of his unconscious ability to find gold. Certain of the motifs and symbols that occur in these novels, for instance, the digging, the retarded child, mental illness, the blind, appear in other of Makanin's works, including *Escape Hatch* and *The Long Road Ahead.* Their meanings extend from one work to another. The work of the reader in interpreting these elements is not unlike the interpretation of dreams. In his analysis of *The Loss,* Peter Rollberg writes: "The composition of this narrative provides the reader with no clear and easy key to its comprehension.... [It] does not stand apart from the complex cluster of epistemological problems explored in the novel, which one intuitively senses as questions of time, death, the formation of myth, and so on. Rather, the composition is part of the *aesthetic realization* of this cluster of issues."[3] The work of making these connections allows the reader to expand his own consciousness, and this is, perhaps, Makanin's response to a culture that imposed meanings on texts to such a grievous extent.

It is not strange, then, that Russian critics and readers of Makanin have argued about how to interpret him, how he fits into the traditions of Russian prose, both classical and Soviet, what his position is on social and political issues. Makanin has given them almost no help. He refused to give interviews to the Soviet press and has stated his opposition to judging writers by any but esthetic criteria.[4] The enigmatic quality of his writing, however, is not explained by the absence of definite social or political or philosophical views; nor does it proceed from a difficult prose style—his prose is quite easy to read. It is puzzling and unsettling in another way, as is the prose of Kafka, for instance, or certain poetry: Makanin challenges us to face our existential fears, our deepest and most agonizing emotional realities—and at a time in history when human institutions seem especially incapable of providing any great hope of salvation. Religious faith, in any conventional sense, provides no consolation in Makanin's texts, and nature is indifferent to man. Although reality in Makanin's works is certainly based in Russian reality and problems are stated in the context of society there, he is interested in processes occurring beneath the social sphere. The investigations take place on a different plane, whatever one chooses to call it—philosophical, spiritual, evolutionary—and they involve human destiny and the way man relates to life processes in the universe. The reader might like more resolution—the endings of both *Escape Hatch* and *The Long Road Ahead* are ambiguous, for example, and strange, but Makanin purposely structures his texts so that interpretations are open-ended.

That man is an element subject to forces of the universe still far beyond his comprehension is the opposite of what was expected from a classical Soviet writer, whose typical hero—a scientist, preferably an engineer—was able to conquer nature and in so doing bring a rather materialistically defined salvation within the reach of human society. The politically correct writer was expected to give the reader moral guidance and correct social and political interpretations. According to the Bolshevik adaptation of Marxist theory, the Soviet Union would evolve into a perfect social system in which the individual would be subordinated to the collective. Makanin responded to this all-too-real cultural pressure by making the repression of the individual in the collective culture one of his major themes. He examines the effects of collective thinking on the individual as well as the responsibilities of individuals to society.

Makanin also explores themes we associate with classical Russian literature—one thinks immediately of Dostoevsky's concern with the meaning of existence, spiritual salvation, questions of good and evil, the effects of science and materialism on the human soul, and so forth. Makanin's texts often allude directly to this tradition. His writings also resemble existential literature in their depiction of the isolated individual, an indifferent, sometimes cruel, universe, the freedom and responsibility of man to choose, and the failures of human reason. There may be a positive future for mankind, but we still don't know how to get there.

In an interview in 1985 Makanin speaks about evolutionary processes: in the period when modern science was developing and religious thought was in crisis, men like Galileo were thought to be crazy and were persecuted. Science gradually gained ascendancy, but in recent times it has entered a period of crisis, for such "advances" as the creation of the atomic bomb have rendered it capable of destroying the world. Figures like the character Yakushkin in *The Precursor* show the need for spiritual rethinking, even if they are quacks. "I think that this is the beginning of humanity's shift from a material to a spiritual system of values," Makanin says, "and perhaps in the 21st century figures of truly great import will appear. In this sense Yakushkin is a forerunner, in this sense Makanin has hope."[5]

Makanin does not write his works with a particular program in mind, however; in the same interview he says that he resists putting his heroes into any existing theoretical system. Nor does he want to moralize, offering instead narratives in which ideas and themes can be explored freely within a basic structure. He often begins with a particular philosophical problem or argument. This approach is illustrated in *The Long Road Ahead*, where, in the narrator's words, "The hero and his (quite ordinary) story were born, one could say, from conversation"–in this instance, a conversation about the evil that dwells within us. Philosophical speculation may provide the idea for a text, but the thoughts are objectified in a reality that is constructed like dreams. In a conversation about Makanin's prose between the critic Karen Stepanyan and the writer Tatyana Tolstaya,[6] Stepanyan says, "You are reading about a life that seems to be completely distant from you but then you feel that you are being told your own dreams. It's like you're at the psychiatrist's." Tolstaya agrees, "It's all like the production of a dream–the way parts are ordered, images are juxtaposed, the key words, certain motifs..."

The dream quality of Makanin's fiction helps to explain its emotional effect. Dreams are true emotionally and seem to contain existential truth, but the material is condensed, metaphorical, oblique and difficult to grasp. Dream thoughts are objectified in dramatic and often visually detailed scenes. Normal perceptions disappear, strange things don't seem strange, natural laws of time and space don't apply. This aura permeates the entire novella *Escape Hatch* and much of *The Long Road Ahead.*

* * *

The original title of *Escape Hatch* is "Laz," from the root "to climb" or "to crawl," which, among other things, means "gap," a passage one can crawl through. The novella focuses on the gap between two worlds, where Klyucharyov is the go-between, the unifying consciousness. Klyucharyov "an old acquaintance of ours," has appeared in several of Makanin's works and is the hero most closely modeled on his own experiences. The name comes from "klyuch," Russian for "key." When asked about Klyucharyov's role as his alter ego, Makanin replied that he was not so much his alter ego as that of an average cultured, educated Russian (*intelligent*), "not too smart," but "not too naive," and that he sometimes referred to his own experience to see how this hero would feel.[7] He's not a hero, but a man. Although not identified here as such, in the story "Klyucharyov and Alimushkin" Klyucharyov is a mathematician at a research institute.

The passage in *Escape Hatch* goes through the earth and Klyucharyov's trips back and forth evoke the struggle of birth. These journeys are physical feats which require the hero to use his intuitive resources and establish contact with the energy of the earth—to "think terrestrially," to "draw on genetic memory." This physical and mental search for origins is important because here Klyucharyov comes face to face with the death of Western civilization, both in terms of material destruction and cultural-spiritual destruction, that is, the loss of language and imaginative thought. On the streets of both worlds people have been deprived of the sustenance of nature, overwhelmed by pavement and high rise buildings in the upper world, and by stores, cafes and artificial lights below. Only when he crawls through the hatch or is digging his cave does Klyucharyov's spirit feel its bond with the earth. He must reassess the human's place in the universe as he struggles to survive on his own.

The two countries in *Escape Hatch* stand in an ironic reversal of the usual position of heaven and hell—the upper one is dark and the lower one light—though good and evil are mixed in both. We are not given any historical or political background; we fall immediately into this reality, as into dream. As a starting point, both worlds emerge from a generalized contemporary Moscow: a materially comfortable cultural elite inhabits the lower world and the upper one, destroyed by poverty and crime, is ruled by an angry and cruel underclass which has lost any sense of civilization. This split universe has been viewed by some as a metaphor for the split in the Russian intelligentsia between those who emigrated to the West in recent decades in search of material comfort and more freedom and those who stayed behind; or the novella is seen as a general apocalyptic portrait of the new Russia, split between the very rich and very poor. There is no single key to this work, however, and I find it more interesting to focus on Makanin's philosophical concerns.

Although the two worlds seem to be separated spatially, it gradually becomes apparent that our ordinary laws of time and space don't apply in *Escape Hatch.* Time doesn't really change, for instance–it's always twilight. And when the hero becomes lost, he's lost in two spaces at the same time–the two worlds are congruent. It's as though the two worlds are not spatially distinct but coextensive in space and time, simply in different dimensions. Their split exists within Klyucharyov's consciousness, too, and at the point when Klyucharyov can no longer mediate between them, both worlds seem doomed. Having lost the ability to communicate with each other, both worlds face extinction. No longer is there "the belief that we are *together* (both there on the dark streets and here at the table), and a belief that this together has been part of our existence from the very beginning..."

The imminent collapse of the upper world is evident from the start; the collapse of the lower world is expressed in the nightmare scene where people return their tickets to the future: "there's been too much blood, you see, and too many tears have been shed, and so we don't believe in it, we have no desire for a future of blood and tears." People are rebelling against the contemporary state of human existence here, too, and they lack an alternative vision.

The scene in which people return their tickets recalls the scene in Dostoevsky's *The Brothers Karamazov,* where Ivan tells Alyosha that he can't forgive God for the torture of children and so he will return his ticket: "Too high a price is asked for harmony; it's beyond our means to pay so much to enter on it. And so I hasten to give back my entrance ticket, and if I am an honest man I am bound to give it back as soon as possible... It's not God that I don't accept, Alyosha, only I most respectfully return Him the ticket."[8]

In *The Brothers Karamazov* Ivan's rebellion is contrasted with the teachings of the monk Father Zosima, who condemns Ivan's rational arguments against God and his materialist rejection of the spiritual world. In what might be seen as a prophecy of Klyucharyov's time, Father Zosima also condemns the idea that freedom consists in the "multiplication and rapid satisfaction of desires." In the rich this leads to "isolation and spiritual suicide; in the poor, envy and murder; for they have been given rights, but have not been shown the means of satisfying their wants."[9] The frightening mob will destroy anything which stands apart from it, but the more individualistic elite has abandoned its responsibility to the rest of humanity.

The splitting of the two worlds in *Escape Hatch* leaves Klyucharyov with no support—material or cultural or spiritual—as his dream about canes for the blind reveals. He has lost the sublime words and comfort of companionship, though he knows these won't help him survive now. His duties lie with his family and friends. Yet the despair of the friends is so great that instinct tells them not to stay together to survive, but "to stay separated, to hide themselves in their nooks... for it is precisely those who have scattered, those who have become like specks of dust, who have the greatest chance to survive and emerge unscathed." In this century Klyucharyov and his family must live apart like the desert monks in the past, turning within to find what part of the human spirit can endure.

* * *

In *The Long Road Ahead* we learn that the young engineer who lives in the future "utopia" has been invented by the narrator and later given to the fragile engineer Ilya Ivanovich, who continues his story. The young hero returns to his creator-narrator only after Ilya Ivanovich's death. The events of the young man's life influence the world of the narrator and Ilya Ivanovich, and vice versa. Synchronicity is an organizing principle in this novella, too. So long as he is under Ilya Ivanovich's watch the young man continues to work at the plant, but after Ilya dies, the young man escapes to the steppe. There he finds other workers who have left the plant. Whereas the young engineer who knew "how to observe from the outside" is at a loss in the steppe, the common people wait calmly and patiently for whatever will come. Although they are scattered physically, they are united, herd-like, in a psychic sense. Unlike the mob in *Escape Hatch* they trust and draw on something within to sustain themselves; but what, if anything, will save them remains to be seen. Two things are clear in this tale, however: the life of an individual cannot be relived and any salvation is far away.

The future society presented here is an extension of our corporate and highly technological world. Makanin questions the idea of technological progress in relation to the nature of humans as a species, in particular our need to use or control other beings. When does killing become evil? If we prohibit our destructive impulses, what happens? How should man relate to other men, to animals, to nature? For some to live according to humanistic values, must others suffer? Can mankind be improved by technology? By art? By love? Why have we failed? These are some of the questions Makanin's texts raise.

The fictional world of the young man can be seen as a metaphor for Russian society, especially in the Soviet period. Makanin satirizes socialist faith in progress, in particular, technological progress, and he explicitly connects the secret system of the slaughterhouse with the secret Gulag prison-camp system. But, again, it is the deeper philosophical and metaphysical concerns that give the novella its energy and force.

The young engineer of *The Long Road Ahead* starts on the road as a socialist realist hero might have some decades earlier, armed with idealism and technological knowledge. On his mission the naive young man enters through the hellish gates of the production-line slaughterhouse and learns about the existence of human evil. He comes as a true believer in humanitarianism and the ability of technology to better people, comparing his invention with the art of Raphael. A product of the competitive corporate world, he tries to save time with his computer analysis. The linear time of the assembly-line is contrasted with time in the non-human universe. When the hero watches the slaughter, however, the knowledge of evil paralyzes him. He chooses to flee, but where to?

Makanin speaks about escape in his interview: "When we became acutely aware of ecological problems and it became clear that the earth is very small, when people suddenly felt the need to fly to other planets, it struck me: My God, it's that same inability to build a life in one's own home—that's what drives them to new places where they think things will be better; although one can predict with certainty that they will mess things up there also.... All the great discoverers forgot about one thing... the kingdom of God is within us...."[10]

Another thing within us, of course, is death. The denial of death is a major factor in the reality we have created for ourselves and another of Makanin's themes. As the narrator and the young engineer show us, art and technology can only create the illusion of resurrection; perhaps a comforting virtual reality can exist, but neither Ilya Ivanovich nor the cows can come back. The playing of the slaughter in reverse is one of the novella's most powerful scenes. To die and to destroy is an integral part of our lives, and the young man rages against this human condition. What can we do but reflect on this and reexamine our selves and our responsibilities in this light? The narrator-creator of the young man on a mission provides an ending which suggests that the common people have insight the young man still lacks, that the simple Olya who understands the cow soul and who loves the hero in a way that is not reciprocated, has more resources than he in the face of death. Do the common people here, who are passive and trusting, rather than angry and destructive, know something more true or are they waiting in vain?

Out of these social and philosophical questions Makanin creates texts which touch us deeply, with the emotional intensity of dreams. His narratives achieve a balance between esthetic freedom and ethical concern. They function as poetry should, in a way similar to that described by Seamus Heaney in his essay "The Government of the Tongue": "... in the rift between what is going to happen and whatever we would wish to happen, poetry holds attention for a space, functions not as distraction but as pure concentration, a focus where our power to concentrate is concentrated back on ourselves."[11]

* * *

It's a pleasure to translate a work that doesn't lose life in rereading. And so I am thankful to the author for these novellas. I am also grateful for the generous help given me by many people from whom I sought advice on particular passages and on the translation as a whole, especially Evgenia Gavrilova, Helena Goscilo, Ronald Meyer, Ellendea Proffer, and Larissa Szporluk.

Cambridge, Massachusetts
October 1995

NOTES

1. An English translation of *Antileader* appears in *The New Soviet Fiction*, ed. by Sergei Zalygin (Abbeville, 1989). *Left behind* appears in *Glasnost: An Anthology of Literature under Gorbachev*, ed. by Helena Goscilo and Byron Lindsey (Ardis, 1990). *Baize-covered Table with Decanter*, translated by Arch Tait (Readers International, 1996), has just been published.

2. In his Foreword to the I Ching.

3. Peter Rollberg, "Invisible Transcendence: Vladimir Makanin's Outsiders," *Kennan Institute Occasional Papers*, No. 253 (Washington, DC, 1993), p. 43.

4. This is mentioned in the interview Makanin gave in 1985 to Peter Rollberg. "Interv'iu Petera Rolberga s Vladimirom Makaninym" in *Odin i Odna* (M.: Russkii iakyk, 1991) 259-77. See also Rollberg, "Invisible Transcendence"; "...golos, letiashchii v kupol," the conversation between Tatyana Tolstaya and Karen Stepanyan in *Voprosy literatury*, No. 2, 1988, 79-105; Natal'ia Ivanova, "Portrety i vokrug (Vladimir Makanin)," in *Tochka zreniia. O proze poslednikh let* (M.: Sovetskii pisatel', 1988), 202-24.

5. Interview with Makanin, 267.

6. Conversation between Tolstaya and Stepanyan, 80.

7. Interview with Makanin.

8. Fyodor Dostoevsky, *The Brothers Karamazov*, trans. Constance Garnett (New York: Macmillan, 1927), 258.

9. Dostoevsky, *Brothers*, 333.

10. Interview with Makanin, 271.

11. Seamus Heaney, quoted in Helen Vendler, "A Nobel for the North," *The New Yorker*, Oct. 23, 1995, 84-89.